"Who?"

To Nicole
My SOS. Sista
Thanks for the support!!
6/1/12

A Delectable Suspense Novel by:
Tiona Pathenia Brown

This work is a work of fiction. It is not meant to depict, portray, or represent any particular persons. All the characters, incidents and dialogues are the products of the author's imagination and are not to be constructed as real. Any resemblance to actual events or person(s) living or dead is purely coincidental.

Creator: *Some people think it's cliché to acknowledge you, but those people don't know the relationship we share. Without a doubt, you're the one who has kept me grounded, who has uplifted me from the debts of insanity and the one who keeps me motivated and I am always blessed. When I was lonely, you were there...when I was afraid, you showed me the light, and when I need you most...you are my best friend. You've never judged me, nor did you allow me to stray too far. I say thank you, over and over again...and I know it's not cliché to acknowledge you, but it's a blessing to praise you and give thanks!!!*

All of you:
Thank you for believing in me and for pushing me to reach goals that I haven't had a chance to set; but yet you saw as necessary accomplishments. Thank you for understanding me, for seeing the strength inside which you pulled out! You said I could do it, you told them I would, and look, I did it!

I write for you, I write for them, and most importantly I write for me.

Where and what would I do without my pen and paper...Sit at my desk and type on the computer. ☺

To my Princess:
You'll never open up one of my books and not see your name there...I love you fatbutt! Always...fyi I'm your friend even when you're not mines!!

To my Prince:
You are the newest addition to our family and you've put a smile inside of mommy and daddy that will never diminish. We love you and welcome you to this crazy family, and one thing is for sure-you'll always know you're loved!!!

Juice:
What doesn't kill us makes us stronger! Do you remember the time when I was down, out, spent, and barely able to see the sun? I sure do and I recall vividly the face of a magnificent angel.

We all make mistakes and have lessons to learn, but know when we get the chance to overcome, to accept and move forward, we must take that opportunity and never look back! You're moving forward and I'm here for you always. Love you!

tt-time:
When you can give from your heart and expect nothing in return, they say that's true giving. Well I expect something from all of us and that's nothing less than greatness because I see the beauty, quality, and ability in us. What do you suppose they call that? I'd say LOVE!

Big Mama:
They may have tried to belittle you, hold you down and make your feel un-pretty. But let me be the one to tell you they have no clue how to break you. The beauty you have is fueled by a heart full of love and they'll never be able to stop you from reaching your true potential.

Ms. Debbie:
You are so genuine and I thank you for helping me; as well as believing in me. Your support will always keep me encouraged. Thanks again.

My Postal Ladies:
Thank you for always putting a smile on my face and making me feel special.

Sonya:
I love that you're a hardcore nerd! You are the coolest and realest person I've met in a long time. Thank you for all you've taught me, for being a great friend, and for meddling here and there; even though it didn't change the outcome. ☺

My King of Hearts:
Divine intervention allowed our paths to cross and I first want to say thank you! Here I was, in my mind, a grown woman who thought she knew a little bit about love, but thank you for showing me a whole lot about sharing love with a man. Deeper than the fairytales, realer than the rain drops on my skin, you put it on me. At first I was scared and unsure of how to react, but you were patient and you taught me to let down my guard and love like never before.

You didn't take advantage of my love...
You asked me to love harder...
You said I should trust...
You promised me nothing more than real love...

With you I learned to love, to dispel the myths and to feel the truth. The hurdles, they were easy to jump because when you're really in love you won't sweat the small stuff. The connection we share is something no one but us can fully understand. What they see is but a fraction of what I feel for you. Hey somebody should tell the big Guy to make more of you

Preface

Bad news sits in my soul and manifests itself into pain, misery, into hopelessness. I wonder each morning will I make it to the afternoon, and in the midday I wonder if I will have the strength to make it to and through the night. I think if I knew *"Who"* did this to me, my life would be easier. I know I could die a happy woman if a name, a face, a body could be identified. Some people can handle situations better when they have all the pieces of the puzzle, and once they've figured things out they can move in a direction that will best suit them. I'm not one of those people…the kind that the *why*, the *where*, or the *how* matters. My mission is solely to solve one piece of this riddle, to find out- *Who?*

Hey, This Is A Suspense Novel; See If You Can Guess Who…Don't Read Ahead☺

Let It Out
Chapter 1

"Hello my name is Kendra. I don't like talking much…well I don't like talking much to strangers, and especially about things I'm embarrassed about. They said it was my turn so I'm going. I'm a single mother of two and I work for the State Liquor Board, but I can't give you any discounts. At times I've been taking it easy, but other days I've found the ground faster than the thoughts of getting out of bed. Each day I think it will get better, but the truth is, each day I think it's getting better is a day I feel I'm closer to the end. I intentionally and continuously struggle to train my mind to think happy thoughts, to see the brighter side, but when I look at my pills or hear a commercial, or see an ad on the back of a bus, I immediately wish someone would just blow my brains out. When I'm inside of my car or my house, I can't even cut on the local radio stations because if I'm remotely in a better mode they could decide to air a *Wrap It Up* commercial. I don't want to feel sorry for myself but I do. I don't want to be embarrassed, but come on now… how can't I? I'm an outcast, some discarded freak of nature…and even if many of you don't see me that way, that's exactly how I see myself. I have to be so careful, to the point that it makes me sick. I'm always on red alert even when Al-Qaeda doesn't make a threat. With my girls I can't let my guard down because I'm so worried about their safety… I wonder how they're really doing and what they're really thinking. I'm sure they're scared to death because I know I am. My family…what they think doesn't matter but who they tell does. I keep asking them to keep my secret, not to tell anyone because I don't want to be treated funny. But I don't trust them because it seems like most of my friends and family have already placed me in the tainted pile, so I'm sure one of them leaked it.

I'm only thirty-two years old, well thirty-two years young-that's what my baby girl would say- and there's so much I wanted to do, so many experiences I wanted to share with my girls. Thirty-two years old and my life should be filled with living, but all I can see is death on my horizon. With each tainted breath I take I can feel the grim reaper's presence, and on the exhale I expect to be laid to rest. I'm all over the place…I'm trying to understand how I'm supposed to overcome this madness when I don't have the answer. I just want to know who did this to me...I want to blame them, yes I do! I know once I know *"Who"* I can move on with my life; well at least I can put that part behind me and see what's left for me. I'm stuck with the perpetrator's three letters but I don't know the perpetrator. I know we're supposed to claim it because it will lighten the load but I don't want to accept this.

My name is Kendra Wright, I'm thirty-two years old, a single mother of two of the best girls born into this world- Kala and Kyra- the most loving and beautiful daughters anyone could have ever asked for, and I'm HIV positive..."

It took a few moments for my mind to realize that my mouth had closed. My face was drenched with tears and my eyes felt heavy. I wasn't free from my anguish, my constant worries or fears, but I'd done something I thought was impossible and for a moment a part of me felt lighter.

Everyone in group started clapping, and I saw a few people clapping while trying to wipe their tears away. There I was, standing in the middle of the Circle of Trust with my counselor Tracy and fifteen group members supporting me through one of the hardest moments in my life. The Circle of Care; which is located at 260 South Broad Street, was referred to me by the counselor who diagnosed me. Initially I thought I'd never show my face (the face of HIV) to anyone, but with the life-altering depression I experience I had no other choice but to get help. In the last few months I went to twenty group meetings and each time I walked through the doors, it felt as if I'd been walking in with cement-block shoes that almost halted my entry into Suite 1000. I often worried about who would see me entering the building and if they knew my purpose for going inside. But once I was in group I had nothing to hide. They understood most of what I was going through because everyone there had the virus, counselors included. However, there was a small distinction between us. They all had something I was searching for. The answer to a question that would take me on a complicated, complex, and life changing two-year journey-*Who gave me this ultimately deadly HIV virus?*

I Love Chocolate
Chapter 2

Every six months my husband Charles and I got tested for STD's, even though we used condoms. He's not the father of my two children. Their biological father Terry, joins the ranks of the many deadbeat dads in the Philadelphia area, and I haven't been able to locate him since the girls baptism; which was over six years ago. Since the deadbeat vanished I have been very selective and apprehensive about bringing any men around my daughters. I've talked to guys on the phone and occasionally went on dates, and although I craved the touch of a man and that long overdue penetration, I didn't want just any ole body around my girls. I promised myself that I would find a good man before I turned thirty and if he didn't show up by then, I'd settle for anything that looked like he could get an erection. Meaning I'd have a boy-toy and only visit him at his place or some other discreet location, when I desired male affection.

Luckily, on a Saturday, while celebrating my twenty-eighth birthday with my cousin Toni at the Olive Garden on Roosevelt Blvd, I met Charles. When I first saw him I told her, "There's my Chocolate Wonder!" Toni laughed before she could even get a good look at him, but when her eyes zoomed in on him she replied, "I might have to taste him first!" Good DNA ran all through this man's blood and he had arms that threw me into an instantaneous daydream. He could definitely lift me. I can't lie my hormones were raging because it had been a while, a long while. What I was most attracted to was his slightly glazed, warm, brown eyes and his inviting smile. I'm not shy-well, not with liquid courage-so I immediately surveyed the area and once I saw no signs of a wife or a girlfriend, I excused myself from the table and walked his way. The fitted, low cut, short black dress I wore made it hard for anyone to miss my curvaceous body, and my stiletto's added three inches to my 5'5 frame, extenuating my perfectly sculpted, toned legs. I felt sexy. No, I radiated sexiness and I needed him to see me, to smell the mouthwatering 'Body' by Victoria's Secret. My scent expressed perfectly what I wanted him to see, taste, and feel...my entire body.

He was standing at the bar drinking a glass of White Zinfandel, and there was no reason or excuse I could use to explain why I had just magically appeared, so I decided to dive right in.

"Hello my name is Kendra and from where I'm sitting it looks like you're lonely."

"Oh it does, does it?" he replied, smiling and showing off his beautiful grin.

"Yes it does, and a fine man like you shouldn't be alone. Are you waiting for someone?"

"Yeah, I'm waiting for someone."

I was so embarrassed! I had made a damn fool of myself. Three to many Long Island Iced Tea's had given me the nerve to approach this good-looking man, and now I wanted to shrink, evaporate, or jump into a time capsule so I could have kept my butt planted at the table with Toni. But it was too late, I had made my move. So my only disappointing option was to push my ego aside and take my behind back to my table, and go home single, horny, and drunk.

Holding my head up high and getting my stiletto's ready to make an about face, he gently caressed my arm and said, "I'm waiting for you." Toni, who had been spying on me and ready to make a move if I didn't, walked past the bar on her way to the restroom. With an amusing smile that danced across her face, she delighted in my achievement as she gave me the thumbs up. This man smelled good, looked good, and dressed in a perfectly cut Italian made suit. Well maybe it came from the discounted chain store The Men's Warehouse. Either way it looked sophisticated and I wanted to know more, see more, and instead of sampling Olive Garden's house wine, I'd taste his lips if I could.

Within twenty minutes, I knew his name, knew he was three years older than me, and that he was recently divorced with no children. For the last eight years he worked at the post office, and his reason for being at the restaurant was to meet his brother and two sisters to celebrate his birthday. Since he had a thing for being early, he figured he would have a few drinks at the bar while he waited for them to arrive. We shared the same birthday, September 12th, and I couldn't believe that I could have possibly met the man of my dreams. Sexy as all hell, employed, no children, no girlfriend or wife, it just didn't get any better than this. Talking to him was effortless and he was a hands-on speaker. Every so often, in the middle of a sentence he would massage my shoulder or slowly caress my left arm; sending chills through my deep-brown-skin, which sent signals to my motherboard that it had been too long! I didn't mind his hands-on approach because it was all welcomed, overdue affection and if he kept it up, I'd have to show him I had hands too. I became so relaxed and in-tune with Charles that I had forgotten all about Toni, who had since guzzled down two more Long-Island's and looked eager to get home because she was barely capable of sitting upright in her seat.

Toni was visiting me from Raleigh, North Carolina and I didn't want to be rude. Well I did but I knew she would never forgive me, so Charles and I exchanged numbers and hugged goodbye before parting ways.

The next week, while I was supposed to be spending time with Toni shopping and doing cousin stuff, I spent most of my time with Charles because he had taken the week off from work. On Monday I called out sick and we went out to breakfast at this comfy little Mom-&-Pop joint in South Philly, then we spent some time at Blinds-To-Go, picking out curtains for his apartment. I know I had only met him two days ago but it felt like I had known him forever. I was so into him and we looked like a real happy couple holding hands, ordering for each other, sneaking kisses in between aisles and enjoying the intimacy of each other. So when he asked me to come over his house and help him hang his curtains, I didn't go all school-girl and act like I would get into trouble if I was alone with him without supervision. Truthfully I wanted to know how much trouble we could get into.

Charles lived in University City, in the mix of the college kids, and when I walked into his house, I was impressed with how well kept his place was. For the most part, single men's homes tend to need a woman's touch, but this man had his stuff together. There were no dirty dish in the sink, and not because he didn't have any dishes, but because he was a clean and tidy man.

Before we started to hang the curtains we sat on the coach, cuddling and discussing our single status.

"Since my divorce I haven't found anyone who I could take serious or that I could trust. I've been married, and I've been single and played games, but I just want a woman who understands commitment and intimacy. I

need someone I can talk to and make love to on many levels."
"When you say levels, what levels are you talking about?"
"Well I should be able to make love to your body and your mind, and in return you should be able to do the same. I don't need someone who just wants a fuck and someone to pay their bills. But don't get me wrong, I'm a provider but I'm more than a superficial fix. I'm in love with love and I want to have a loving woman who I can share my world with. What do you think?"
"I think I'm ready to share some things with you..."
"Like what?"
"I wasn't talking about sex Charles."
"Well, why did you bring it up?"

I started laughing because sex was all over my mind. I didn't want to seem easy but he was saying all the things I wanted to hear. Could I have sex with him on our first real date and still have his respect? It had been two long- did I say long-years but I wanted his respect. I wanted to ask him his opinion on women who gave it up quickly but before I could, he laid me back onto the coach and took my shoes off. Then he delicately kissed my lips. I wanted to jump out of my clothes but I felt he might just have wanted to kiss, so I kissed back. Then he stopped me unexpectedly.
"Look at me." He demanded.
"I am..."
"No, I want you to look into my eyes."
"Charles I am" I softly replied, staring keenly into his warm glazed brown eyes.
"I'm going to make love to your body and you're going to do the same to me." He stated, boldly and without doubt.

"Stand up first, I want to see you."
"Ok" I said, without hesitation as I began slowly modeling my physique for him.
"Kendra you're beautiful…Come closer." He slowly removed my fitted black jeans, as I slid off my socks. And when he went to remove my black-lace thong, he turned me around and gently started kissing and sucking the bottom of my right cheek. I wanted those panties off and the dick in, but he made me wait. He knew how to initiate and apply foreplay but I was going through withdraw symptoms and I needed my fix.

By the time he took my sweater and bra off I had the shakes. I was trembling and I wanted the antidote. Then he instructed me, "Come undress me" and of course I didn't have a problem with that. His clothes off meant I was one step closer to my deep chocolate treat. Charles was standing with his shirt and jeans off, and I went to remove the briefs that held the key to what I'd been craving for the last two years. However, before I began to pull them down, I took a good look at the preview and his imprint assured me I was going to get something out of this deal.

Now I didn't want to rush. I wanted to take my time and show him some of my skills. This was my moment to provide him with a foreplay delight. So I tickled his lower half with my lips and soothingly blew warm kisses through his briefs. Then I took my pointer finger and showed him what my juicy lips and warm mouth could do, until he begged me to take his briefs off. Finally they were off and I had a complete view of the man that I was going to give full control over my body.

He was a masterpiece, each part of him perfectly sculpted and his chocolate dick was calling me. I wanted to gobble it down, so I did. It was so much more than I had first calculated, but I was a woman who had more to offer than he knew. "Wow", was all he could say as I gave this man the best lip-to-dick action he had ever felt. I felt his yearning to cum but instead of giving in he said, "Now it's my turn" as he picked me up and carried me into the bedroom. He laid my anxious body down and brushed his nose up against my D's and quickly got acquainted with my nipples. Then he made his descend and his mouth greeted my clitoris as if they had been best friends, knowing each other's wants to a tee. I kept pulling back because I couldn't control myself, I couldn't handle it, but he kept placing me in the position he wanted me in, constantly telling me, "You can handle it." The sounds alone of him suckling and slurping my pussy were bringing me to tears. He put my hands on his head and I massaged his scalp and squeezed when I felt I was about to blow. Then he asked, "Do you like it?" Was he kidding? I loved it and he could tell from the river that was flowing into his mouth. Without warning he leaned over and went into his nightstand and grabbed a Trojan, Extra- Thin & Sensitive in a deep purple wrapper. Then he placed it in my hands, lifted my chin up so we could be eye level, and said, "Put it on your dick." He could taste my anticipation with each breath I took. My heart was racing and my body temperature had risen. I'm sure it felt as if I was feverish but I wasn't sick, just in need of his stick.

I couldn't get it opened fast enough and my hand seemed like it had a built in razor-blade because I got the wrapper open on my first attempt. While I rolled the condom down onto his Mr.Good-Bar, he kept looking into my eyes. Once it was finally on, he assertively said, "Brace yourself, impact will occur shortly." With just the tip inserted, I felt like a virgin and once fully breached there was an explosion! He angled himself perfectly and stroked my g-spot with accurate precision. Just by the way he touched my body and ran his hands through my hair, made me feel as if I was in love. Each stroke brought me closer to a feeling I vaguely remembered but my memory was quickly going into total recall.

"Kendra, look at me. Can I go deeper?" Charles asked.

"Charles go as deep as you want!" As soon as I answered he thrust himself deeper inside my walls.

"Kiss me" he said, and of course I passionately did.

In that moment he could have asked me to walk to Geno's in my birthday suit and bring him back a cheese steak, with extra onions, light mayo, ketchup on the right side of the roll, bread slightly toasted, with two thin sliced pickles, and not only would I have complied but I would have gotten his order exact. This was a chocolate lover's dream, a rare experience for me and he had my body and my mind. He lifted up both of my robust legs and I didn't feel like a big girl. I kept inching them down. Charles was a lot! But he wanted my legs up, so I took deep breaths as he went deeper and deeper, causing my pussy to pant and clutch, and cling onto his mighty cylinder. I was ready. I could feel it coming and I wasn't trying to hold it in any longer.

"Oh my world this is really happening!"

"Yes it is Kendra…Kendra!"

"Oh Charles, Thank You, Thank You…Uhhhmmmmmmm!"

It was a real orgasm. Not the kind where you shake your cum out and wiggle your legs around, just to make your partner think he did something. But the kind that comes from the base of the spine to the top of your head, through the pussy down to your toes, and totally controls your central nervous system; then relaxes each muscle and makes the body feel weightless, satisfied, and ready for bed. Yes the sun was still up but my body was ready for a complete shut-down.

For a moment I began to feel bad because I didn't think Charles had cum. I was so caught up in my own experience but when I slightly lifted my up head, I saw him cleaning himself off and there was an abundance of sperm in the condom. It's something when two people can orgasm at the same time, and it's certainly something I had never experienced before. But it was definitely a feeling I wanted to explore more often; because how great is it for both parties to win a prize at the same time? Charles and I cuddled and talked briefly because as I lay on his chest, while he caressed my body and held me tight, I dosed off.

Around four 'o' clock A.M., I was awakened to the sound of my cell phone ranging and I knew it had to be Toni. At first I ignored her but she kept calling so I thought maybe something was wrong with the girls. My body was still worn-out but I lifted myself up and made my way to the coach to get my phone out of my pocketbook.

"Hey Toni, what's wrong?"

"What's wrong?"

"Yes, what's up?" I said sensing some tension in her voice.

"Who did I come up here to see?" She stated sarcastically.

"Girl I know you're not trippin. You're here all week." I said, hoping my response would reassure her I'd make time for her.

"So I'm trippin…no you trippin! I told you I ain't gonna be no back-burner chick for no one."

"Toni I think you need to calm down and just ease up." I tried whispering because I didn't want Charles to hear me.
"Yeah I'm going to ease up, right the hell out of here!"
She hung up on me but I wasn't surprised because Toni and I had a very rough relationship. Our problems went all the way back to the tender age of five years old.

My Aunt Kelly, her mother, and my mom Debbie, are really close and had given birth to us three months apart. Toni's older and we could never see eye to eye. When I was five she spent the Christmas holiday over my house and on Christmas morning she got upset because my mom had bought me this Barbie doll that Toni had wanted. So later that night she painted my Barbie's face and body with red nail polish, cut off her hair and took all my new Barbie clothes and poured the remainder nail polish on them. When I woke up the next day I cried all day and my mom made some excuse for her and no one chastised her. They kept saying she suffered from the only child syndrome, and I'm still wondering what that means because I'm an only child as well but I never pulled stunts like that. Aunt Kelly overly spoiled her and she's always been a brat. Just being in the same family with her was extremely challenging but going to school with her was the biggest headache of my life.

Toni was always in competition with me, trying to beat my grades, dress better, and it got really bad when she applied and got accepted to the same high school I was attending, Central. Being in elementary and middle school together was okay but I was fed up with her. I thought I had finally gotten rid of this girl but she was like an unshakable groupie. Always following me around and wanting to be like me. It was aggravating and not the least flattering. Then senior year she just so happened to like the guy I was dating. This was strange, because we all know there's and unspoken rule that your boyfriend, man, or husband is strictly off limits to your friends and especially your family. But Toni never got that memo. She wrote the words whore and back stabber, in permanent black marker, repeatedly on my locker and spread malicious lies about me throughout the school. It even got physical on prom night because she thought her lies would have made my boyfriend, Rich- now try to figure this one out- leave me and be her prom date.

So after prom, my two friends and their dates, Toni and her date, and Rich and I went to the Melrose diner in South Philly to eat breakfast. She kept eyeing Rich and it was so obvious that he whispered in my ear and asked what was up with her. I didn't know what to tell him but it became so annoying and everyone knew something was up, so I asked her to walk me to the bathroom. As soon as we got in the restroom I blurted out, "Why do you keep looking at him?" She couldn't wait to respond, it was at the tip of her mouth almost leaping off of her tongue.

"Because he's with a whore and I'm trying to understand why he would want your ugly ass over me!" Toni had taken this to another level. She had always been mean and did things out of spite, but to call me a whore...I'd never thought I would see the day. Especially since she was the one with quite the reputation and I was still a virgin. When I looked into her eyes there was this evil glaze coming off of her darkened pupils and I just wanted to get away from her, so I made my way back to the table. But she quickly walked right behind me and repeated her exact statement to me in front of everybody.

Everyone was shocked and her date, the one who had driven her to the diner, got up and stormed out. His exit was just what she deserved and as I begin to take my seat, I laughed at her and said, “So who’s going to take you home now?” No sooner than I had closed my mouth Toni punched me in my face so hard that I can still remember seeing stars and feeling dizzy. We started fighting and I want to say I won, but she fought with this crazy strength and it was hard to get control over her. Rich let us tussle for a bit, because he didn’t like her and wanted me to kick her ass, but when he realized she was getting the best of me he broke us up. My entire night was ruined! I was embarrassed and as Rich drove me home I cried and told myself she was dead to me, cousin and all.

Of course our mothers, who were so close thought that we should be tight as sisters too, tried like hell to patch things up between us. The funny part is I kept allowing them to fix up our relationship, which was obviously irreconcilable. Toni was just a constant migraine and an attempt to try and please my mom and my auntie by staying friends with her was too big of a burden on me. And now, with this irate phone call from her, I clearly recalled why I was so excited when she moved out of the city five years ago.

I didn’t want to leave Charles but I had no other choice. So I woke him up to let him know I was going home to check on the girls. I didn’t trust Toni; she might have set the house on fire, with her, who knows. And just my luck she’d get away with it by claiming she was bi-polar. Yes, she had self-diagnosed herself and my mom and my aunt believed that was why she was emotionally unstable, but never wanted her medicated. They said it would eat away at her brain. But from what I could see something was already gnawing at it, so anything was worth a try to get her to some level of normalcy.

Charles didn't want me to go and asked if I could stay a little longer, but even though I wanted to stay I couldn't because my girls were only 10 and 7. I wasn't going to leave them in the house with Toni because she obviously didn't want to babysit any longer. Charles was under the impression that Toni was there and would continue to watch them but since he was asleep he didn't hear our brief argument. I quickly made up a story about Toni having to make an emergency run and told him that I hoped this wouldn't be our last night together. He grinned and playfully said, "No…unless you're done with me." So for now we ended our night with a passionate kiss then I hurried home.

When I got there Toni was sitting on the coach watching TV with the girls, and when I walked in she didn't even turn her head in my direction. I stared at her because for one it was damn near six in the morning so why were the girls still up, and secondly as calm and as comfortable she was with them, what was the problem with her watching them a little while longer? She continued watching TV as I greeted the girls with kisses and hugs, and then I asked them to go to their bedrooms while I had an adult talk with their Aunt Toni. Once I heard their bedroom doors closed I confronted her.

"Toni, what's your problem?

"Problem solved."

"Okay, so why are you still here?"

"Because I wanted to see you before I left."

"Okay…Were you going to leave the girls here by themselves?"

"No. If you didn't get here before I was ready to go, you were going to leave them by themselves… and I would have had no other choice but to call social services."

"You really got some damn nerve; I mean you really are crazy! Did you take your medicine today!" I said as I balled up my fist because she was truly testing me.

"Yeah I did, did you get some medicine today?" she asked, as she giggled.

"Toni I'm grown and I'm living my life for me not you. Don't concern yourself with me because I'm no longer concerning myself with you. This relationship is toxic and I'm tired of feeling as though I did something wrong, when the truth is I don't owe you shit and never have."

"So you want me out…" she asked as she began nodding her head up and down as if she had just come to understand something that had been plaguing her for the longest.

"Yes I do!"

"After I drove almost eight hours up here to spend time with my favorite cousin?" She wasn't smiling anymore and she started to get that crazy look in her eyes.

"Favorite what? I told you before that I'm tired and fed up with you and from this day on we ain't family. You're nothing to me, dead matter and you don't matter!"

"Bitch you better take that shit back and stop frontin on me! I got my stuff packed but I knew you were going to apologize when you walked in that door, and there's still time!" She crossed her arms and patiently waited for my apology.

"You right…there's still time for you to get out my house!"
"If I leave here I'm never coming back and I don't want you to call me anymore about being lonely and how bad you want a man. And I'm going to make sure Aunt Debbie knows how badly you treated me! You put a piece of meat over me…and you know how I can get too!" She said sharply.
"I don't care how you can get! What the hell are you getting at…you tryin to fight?"
She stared but didn't respond and I knew in her mind she felt she could beat me without much effort.
"Listen I'm not gonna fight you, just get out of my damn house!" I yelled.
"Kendra I hate you…And I promise you I won't be there for you if you don't apologize!"
"Are you still breathing? Well if you're waiting for an apology you'll die before you get it!"
"I'm going to make sure you die Bitch!" Toni snapped. Her eyes were dead serious.
"Toni I hate you too…Have a nice life!"

I might have taken her seriously but she had threatened to kill me several times before, and for the smallest things. Like the time I forgot to get her a Pepsi when I went to the Chinese store to pick up our take-out. Toni's behavior was pathetic and I'd had enough. It had been something we'd gone through our entire lives and this time our mothers would have no say. Once she was walked out of my front door I'd never call or ask about her again. It was time she dealt with some consequences from me, and eliminating her seemed to be the only way to make her see I didn't have to put up with her shit.

On her way out of the door she dropped and broke the teacup she held in her hand, but besides that she left without any further physical incident to anything or anybody. She got in her gold Honda Accord and sped off. I saw her circle the block a few times and she was driving so fast that her Hawaiian-hula bobble head doll looked like it was about to topple off the dashboard. On rare occasions, she has come to her senses and apologized, so I momentarily thought she was circling the block working on an explanation. But it soon became clear I wouldn't be getting one today. Then like some teenaged nut she played on my phone. The second time she called I answered and she spewed profanity and made her threats, so I hung up the phone and silenced the ringer, but she continued to call for a good twenty minutes.

Once things were quiet I went into the girls' room to make sure they were sleeping. I went into my bedroom and lay back on my bed thinking of how less stressed my life was when Toni wasn't in it, and I wanted to keep it that way. It was time to live in the present and I wanted to focus on satisfying my sexual desires and seeing if Mr. Good-Bar was more than just a first-class lay.

Give Him A Chance...Please
Chapter 3

Our relationship developed rather quickly, and I made the difficult choice to allow him to meet my daughters after dating him for only a month. Since the girls couldn't remember the last time a man was in our house, other than a relative, I decided we'd meet him at Friendly's. I tried to find the right way to ask if they wanted to meet Charles because I was skeptical and scared of their reply, but I stayed hopeful and after we finished diner I asked them.

"Girls I know this may come as a surprise but I met a really, really nice guy and he wants to meet you." I screened their faces waiting on a response.

"I don't have a problem with that mom, you're pretty so why not." Kala said, and that was surprising because she's always so protective. Whenever men tried to talk to me at the Laundromat or grocery store, she'd stand there and look at them like they were silly. Kyra, my youngest who never went against any of my suggestions wasn't smiling and said, "I don't want to go." Her reaction made me question myself. I didn't want to be selfish but at the same time I didn't want to let them run my entire life.

"Why not Kyra?" I said disapprovingly.

"Because I don't like him".

"But you haven't even met him yet?"

"I know." She smiled and looked at me as if we were done the conversation.

I had seen her try this stunt before, where she'd figure I'd give in because she smiled and said she didn't feel like or want to do something. I'll admit I'm guilty of spoiling my girls because of the guilt I carry around raising them without a father or father figure. Both my girls attend Greene Street Friends Private School and receive an excellent education. They have so many clothes that they outgrow some items before they even get to wear them. I've taken them out of the country twice and to Disney land every year for the past three years, both of them have savings accounts and college funds, and they don't want for anything. But this time… I want to be spoiled.

"Kyra I'm going to take you with us and after we eat, if you don't like Mr. Charles we will talk about it then…Ok?"

"Mom, I don't want to go!" I saw a tear roll down her bronze cheek and I wasn't sure why she was overreacting, but I assured her that she was going. I figured if they didn't like him at least they could get a good sundae out of this whole ordeal. But I wanted them to at the very least, give him a chance because he was so good to me.

When we entered the restaurant Charles was waiting for us and he quickly introduced himself to my oldest Kala. He gave her a handshake and Kyra came up out of nowhere and gave him a hug. It was an awkward moment for me because I'd never seen Kyra so comfortable with any guy, and her behavior at the dinner table the previous night had me believing she was going to pull a tantrum. For the moment I had to be a little suspicious of her because she might have been trying to pull a fast one, but for now I was happy.

By the time desert came I knew he had won the girls over. Charles had a wonderful sense of humor and a way of making you feel very comfortable. At one point the girls were too comfortable. When Kyra said, "My mom hasn't had a man in a long time but you seem good for her." I was so embarrassed and ready to pull the drawstrings of my hoody together until my face had disappeared, but I felt at ease when he replied, "She is very beautiful and any man would be blessed to have such a great woman in his life." I blushed and smiled. It had been a long time since I received such a compliment and it was more extraordinary because he was speaking so highly of me in front of the girls. As the family date progressed, the girls had honed all their attention on Charles and I simply sat back and enjoyed seeing them smile and giggle.

When the table was cleared, Charles paid the bill and gave the girls a lesson on how to leave a proper tip, and then he walked us to the car. He was his usual self, opening the car doors for the girls and making sure they buckled up. Then he gave me a hug and a quick peck on the cheek before I got in the car and drove off. As we approached the first red traffic light Kyra was eager to let me know how nice she thought Mr. Charles was, and she asked when she was going to see him again. Kala agreed, saying he was pretty cool and suggested that I see him more often. Charles had made a great impression on my girls and that only made me fall for him even more.

A week after the get together with the girls, Charles asked me to meet him so we could discuss the future of our relationship. I was nervous because we hadn't talked much after that night and I hadn't seen him at all, but I wanted to meet up so I could find out why he was avoiding me. If he tried to break up with me because he couldn't handle the fact that I had kids, I'd have to go in my bag and show him another side of me. But for now I called my cousin Keyona to come over and keep an eye on the girls. Not only was she good with the girls but she was responsible and she was family. She attended Community College of Philadelphia, while she tried to get her GPA up before transferring to Temple University; and being a freshman, without a job, she was always looking for babysitting gigs.

When I got to the door of Charles' apartment it was very quiet and there was a note on the door with my name on it.

Hi baby. When you come in go straight to the bathroom and remove all articles of clothing. Don't cut on the lights… Love you Charles

It was very dark inside of his apartment and as I walked into the living room and down the hallway, past the bedroom door to the bathroom, I was anxious to see what awaited me. Charles was a big romantic and he's showered me with flowers, candy, and candle-lit dinners but this note-play was different. I had no clue what to expect when I entered the bathroom but I had every attention of finding out, so I followed my instructions to the tee. When I entered the bathroom, tea-light candles were strategically placed all around and a red and white rose pedal bubble bath was drawn. I obeyed the instructions in the first letter and quickly removed all of my clothes then I proceeded to read the letter that was taped onto the bathroom mirror.

You've had a long day, you deserve a good soak. Ease in and I'll be in momentarily.

Charles knew how much I loved his tub. It was the perfect size for the two of us and it had plenty room to relax and soak among other activities. The warm water was the perfect temperature and when it caressed my flesh, I was instantly relaxed but ready for my man as well. Work had drained me because my new promotion as District Manager had me all over the city, dealing with employee's problems, customer issues and creating resolutions to stay within the new budget. With my eyes closed and a feeling of tranquility flowing throughout my body, a smile came across my face because this was just like Charles. I didn't know how long it would take him to enter the bathroom, but I was happy to play his game.

When I heard the door smoothly slide open, the first image I saw was of Charles in his birthday suit, and as usual he was happy to see me. He had a bath sponge in one hand and a glass of red wine in the other, and he made sure to tell me to hold tight. By now he knew that I found it difficult to keep my hands off of him, but I knew that he wanted me to relax so I chilled. He slid in the tub behind me and began stroking my body with the soft fibers of the sponge. With no music playing I enjoyed the silence in the room. It gave me a chance to hear each word he softly spoke into my ear, the sounds of the water, and the words that instantly turned the night into overdrive "bend-over".

I leaned over the oversized tub and the first stroke was more than enough for me to reach an orgasm. I was already at my peak because he mentally stimulated me with each word he whispered and him pampering my body made this one effortless. After he had his way with me in the tub, we dried each other off with the plush bath towels that he had laid out before he led me into the bedroom. He kept all the lights out and before he opened the bedroom door I could see the glow of flickering candle lights.

Once inside I was in awe by the amount of roses impeccably positioned around the room, and the scented amber-rose candles were a perfect touch. Quickly I glanced in the mirror at my disheveled shoulder length, dark brown hair. With Charles I was so use to him messing up my hair that I decided after tonight it would be smarter if I got me some micro braids. At least I'd save time trying to fix my hair in the mornings for work, and he could get my braids wet and pull them, or do whatever he wanted to them without any complaints from me. Charles knew I always wanted to look good for him so he said, "Your hair looks just fine." Then he held my hand as he led me to his king-size bed and I saw another note. I went to pick it up but he said, "Baby let me read this one." Then he sat me on the bed and kissed me intensely before reading the message…

Kendra what I feel for you cannot be contained. Ever since I met you, I've been living the life that I want to live for the rest of my life. Are you willing to stay in my life now and forever as my wife…Will you marry me?

Daddy's Home
Chapter 4

Two months after the proposal, on December 15th 2006, we got married at Enon-East Baptist Church on Coulter Street in Germantown. It was everything I wanted and everything I could have ever dreamed of. The perfect dress, the flawless emerald cut ring, and the prettiest flower girls-my babies of course. From every corner of the church you could see white rose flower arrangements, with a touch of baby's breath, and my cousin Keyona, with her raspy voice, was kind enough to sing my mom's favorite song as I walked down the aisle, "*At Last*" by Etta James. My aunt Kelly was my matron of honor and only member of my bridal party and Charles' brother Spade was his best man. We kept our wedding party very small because Charles wanted it that way. This was okay by me because if he had asked me to go to the Justice of the Peace, I would have done it that way too; but this way was much better! All of our family and friends were dressed in black and white. At first I got a lot of backlash, because everyone thought only the bride should wear white, but the colors scheme added a level of sophistication to our affair.

As I anxiously walked down the aisle with my father Roosevelt, standing before me was a dream that I never imagined would be my reality. Before Charles entered my life I was sure all good men had disappeared but now I had the perfect man! Since meeting Charles I had been on cloud nine and our marriage just assured me how real this was. No more lonely nights, praying for a man, or burning out the batteries in my rabbit and silver bullet…I had found my soul mate.

Our ceremony was the most immaculate and everything worked out perfectly, without any flaws. I was pleased to have received all those hefty envelopes, which would be used to help us do a little home redecorating. Instead of buying a new place, my husband and I decided we'd stay in my four bedroom, two full bath home in Wynnefield, on the 2300 block of Georges Lane. The area is considered a middle class suburb and it's beautiful, more importantly it was paid for. I inherited the home and several thousand dollars from my grandfather when I turned twenty-one. At first I wanted to sell the house and spend, splurge and spend, but thanks to the guidance of my father I didn't ruin my inheritance.

Many of my family members weren't too pleased at my grandfather's choice to leave me such a substantial inheritance and even I didn't understand why he left it to me. I wasn't particularly close to any of my family members, including my grandfather who I only visited once during his agonizing three year battle with lung cancer; which ultimately led to his death. I was not a fan of hospitals and never had the stomach for seeing him vomit, let alone the disgusting and terrible stomach turning tribulations he was going through. But whatever his reasoning, he left the inheritance to me and I was extremely grateful because I loved my home! It was a peaceful and safe neighborhood and now the perfect home had the perfect family.

Charles was everything I wanted and he did anything to please me. He cooked and he cleaned. Actually he was a neat freak-who wanted everything in its place- but so was I, which was a big relief to me. Every morning before he went to work, he dropped the girls off at school and helped them with their homework when he got home. He even did most of my household chores…washing dishes and doing laundry. Also he kept his promises! Instead of us going on a honeymoon he promised to get me something much better, and he did. I had been eyeing the 07' BMW X5 and he delivered on his promise two weeks after we were married. I was rushing out the house to get to work and my dream car was in front of the door, red bow attached with a heart shaped note-that read…

There's nothing too good for my wife…Love Daddy!!!

Thankfully Charles was very good with saving and making money because he only added to our life and made it more enjoyable. The idea of having a great man who is broke just seems like you're being cheated, but with Charles I had no worries. He had A-1 credit and had learned a thing or two about the stock market. I had tried to figure it out, but when he explained things to me it all seemed like gibberish, so he stopped trying to force those lessons on me. We had joint bank accounts and even though he had a good twenty thousand dollars more than me, he gave me full access to it. It's a wonderful feeling to have the trust of the man you love and cherish, and my mom always said if a man gives you full access to his money then he really loves you.

After six months of bliss, the only thing missing from our lives was a baby. Charles loved my children and treated them as his own but I could see the craving for him to have one of his own. I had no intentions of denying my husband from his desire because we both were financially and emotionally capable of providing for a child, and we both enjoyed being parents. Without hesitation I took the blame for not immediately getting pregnant because I had been on the Depo-Provera shot for the last three years, and it was slowly removing its anti-baby serum from my body. At first, Charles was confused when I tried to explain to him my reasons for staying on Depo especially since I hadn't been sexually active for at least two years prior to meeting him. I did my best to assure him that I wasn't lying and to give him some clarification.

I initially got on the shot because when I slept with my ex Kumar, the condom broke. For me it was one of the most terrifying moments I had endured, because I didn't want to be a single mother again. So once I got on the shot, I never got off of it until we got married. Maybe I was addicted because every three months I went faithfully to see Dr. Robinson for my injection. I loved the shot because it eliminated my menstrual cycle and the only side-effect I encountered was the thinning of my hair. My edges were paper thin for some time and then they grew back in fuller within the first year of me getting the shot. But now this once loved birth control method was irritating the hell out of me because I wanted to get pregnant as soon as I stopped my injections. However, a couple of weeks after I stopped getting the Depo I bleed for thirty days straight. Not spotting, but a full period for thirty days and I thought I was going to need a complete hysterectomy. When I went to see my doctor she said this was normal, just a rare side-effect (which somehow was normal) of the Depo. Had she told me about that rare side-effect and the drugs ability to stay in my system for God knows how long, I would have never taken it in the first place. Especially since I hadn't had any sex for such a long period of time between my last encounter with my ex and Charles. There was really no need for me to be on a '*just in case*' dose.

Now six months after my wedding day, not only was I not expecting but now I had this itchy abnormal discharge that needed to be brought to my doctor's attention immediately. I made an appointment at the City Line Family Medicine facility. Since I didn't work weekends unless it was an emergency, I made an appointment on Saturday because we were saving all our vacation days to go on a Disney World cruise in July. So on a sunny and breezy June day, I sat in the dimly lit doctor's office until I was called in the back by the medical assistant to see my doctor.

Upon entering the exam room my doctor was already there. When she wasn't busy she'd often triage me and it made me feel lucky to have a doctor who'd take the time to give you that extra one-on-one care. So I was all delighted to see her warm smile when I came in to the room.

"Hi Dr. Robinson."

"Hello, Kendra, what seems to be the problem?" she said as she began to write down the reason for my visit.

"I'm having this discharge and it's itchy and irritating. I guess it's another side effect of the Depo. I swear I really want this stuff out of my body so I can add an addition to my family."

"Okay, let me take your temperature and get your blood pressure" she said, as she placed the thermometer under my tongue and wrapped the blood pressure cuff around my upper arm.

"Sure, I'm in no rush," I replied.

"What color is the discharge?" she asked, as she began to jot down my results.

"It's white...and a little thick. I think it's probably a yeast infection and I was going to buy an over the counter cream, but since I'm dealing with the Depo drama I figured it would be better to have you take a look."

"It's always better to play it safe. Why don't you get undressed and I'll be right back in to examine you. Go ahead and take everything off. Since you're here I'll do a breast exam as well."

She handed me the standard thin backless blue paper gown and as soon as she left the room I began to undress. Within five minutes she returned and began the breast examination and she didn't' feel any lumps. This may sound weird but when she began my GYN examination I was excited. I enjoyed them because they tickled and stimulated my g-spot. . I always contained myself and never gave any indication that I was having a great time, and if I didn't have to pay the seventy-five dollar co-pay to Etna for each doctor's visits, I probably would have tried to get two pap's a year.

"Okay Kendra you can sit up and here are some paper towels so you can wipe yourself off. Give me a sec and I'll be right back, and go ahead and get dressed."

I was relived to put my clothes on because it was freezing in that office. But my relief was short lived because when she re-entered the room she sat on the doctor's chair and asked, "Have you or your husband had sex with anyone new?" I was puzzled, and when she said anyone new, I thought, yeah me and him are new. But what did she mean by new? I didn't feel like trying to figure out where she was going inside my head, so I blurted out,

"What's the problem?"

"Kendra you have Chlamydia."

I had never had a sexual transmitted disease in my entire life and now she was saying I had Chlamydia.
"How do I have Chlamydia? I'm not sleeping with anyone but Charles and he's not sleeping with anyone either!" I was frustrated and I wanted her to re-do the test. It had to be a mistake. I just married the man of my dreams. I was only here to get treated for a yeast infection, not an STD.
"Kendra you can never really know what someone is doing. If you haven't been with anyone, then maybe your husband has. Charles needs to be tested. I'm going to write you a prescription for Doxycycline. You take one twice a day for a week and you'll be fine."
"No I won't be fine…"
"I understand that this is very frustrating but it's better to know and make sure you stay healthy. While we're here, I'd like to test you for HIV..."
"HIV!"
"Yes, because the last time you were tested was over four years ago."
I didn't want to be tested for HIV because I didn't have it. I had only been with Charles and if I had HIV…well that didn't matter because I didn't have it. Suddenly I felt lifeless, dead before any test results had been given, dying before the test had even been taken.
"Dr. Robinson I don't have HIV so why would I get tested?"
"Kendra, I'm not saying you have it, I just want to test you for it. It's an option and you don't have to take the test. I just want you to have the facts. HIV isn't a death trap and there are medications that ensure those infected have a full life."
"I don't have HIV!" I yelled as I began standing in the small room and pacing in the tight corner.

"Again I'm not saying that you do", she said as she placed her hand on my shoulder to comfort and calm me. "Do you want to take the test?" she repeated.

I couldn't even look into her eyes. My neck felt so strained... as if my head was so heavy that my neck couldn't carry the weight and my heart ached. If Charles had given me Chlamydia and possibly HIV, what would I do? A pill could fix my Chlamydia infection but there was no pill that could erase an HIV curse. Dr. Robinson was patient and I finally decided that for my girls I needed to know.

"Yes I'll take the test, how long before I know my results."

"Usually within five to seven days."

"Why so long?"

"That's standard time?"

"So there's nothing sooner?"

"Yes, they have rapid salvia test where you can get the results within twenty minutes. But we don't have that option here. We do a blood test and send the sample off to the Lab."

"Is the rapid test accurate...I mean does it work better than a blood test?"

"They both have accuracy rates of 99.5%. If you want to get a rapid test they have free centers around the city, and you'll get the results within twenty minutes. I have a list of locations I can give you."

"How private is it?"

"The results are not shared and it's a confidential matter, just as if you were to take the test here."

God forbid I did have HIV; I didn't want anyone to know that I did. This was supposed to be a simple doctor's visit with a prescription for Monistat, not a death sentence. I wanted to call Charles. No, I wanted to kill him! Even if I didn't have HIV I damn sure had Chlamydia and that only meant one thing-he was sticking his Mr. Good-Bar in another pot of chocolate.

I decided to get the list of rapid testing centers and visit one of the locations because I couldn't take the agony of waiting for the damn results. If I was dying I wanted to know immediately. There were over ten testing centers in the Philadelphia area but only two were open on Saturdays, between the hours of noon and four. It was already two 'o' clock P.M., and the nearest center was Washington West on 12th and Locust Streets. So I drove down I-76 to that center. Charles called my cell phone while I was driving but I didn't bother answering. He had the girls so they were okay and my mind was only focused on finding out what I did or did not have, and then dealing with Charles later. I tried to think positive but that wasn't working. Images of my dead, decrepit body and my casket kept flashing before my eyes, and even though I wasn't a crier, when the thought of dying and leaving my girls without their mother entered my mind I broke. I was sobbing so deeply I could barely see the cars in front of me and the nerves inside my stomach had morphed into tigers that were ripping my stomach a part.

Downtown was crowded and congested and I couldn't find a parking spot anywhere. Also every driver pissed me off. I had never used so much profanity in my life but each driver who cut me off or wouldn't let me change lanes, got some choice words and a few middle fingers. One guy had the nerve to give me this crazy stare after he cut me off, so I pulled beside him and motioned for him to roll his window down. Instead of rolling down the window he laughed in my face. When the light turned green, he waved goodbye and drove away. I started to follow him but I realized I was tripping and was possibly about to get my butt shot, so I calmed down and got back on track.

I finally found a parking spot five blocks away and made my way to the center. Each step felt like an eternity and I thought about turning back. I kept asking myself, "Do I really need to know"? But I knew I had to know. It would not be right as a woman and a mother, not to know what was going on inside of my body. The closer I got to 12th Street the more I panicked. I wondered if I would see anyone I knew from work or a family member or friend. Then I questioned if they would tell anyone. It was enough to make me turn around but I forced myself to walk into the automatic doors of Washington West.

The center was a clinic where they did free testing for all STD's and they also had family planning there; which made me feel a little better because the four people in the waiting area didn't have to know the exact reason for my visit. When I walked to the counter I was met by a very polite receptionist named Cinnamon. On a normal day, I would have found her name amusing. She wasn't a stripper but Cinnamon was her real name, but today I wasn't in the mood. She softly asked me "What brings you in today?", and I nervously looked around to see if anyone was watching me. I sure didn't want someone to hear me, so I whispered, "I'm here for a rapid test." She responded, "Oh, I'm sorry I didn't hear you. What did you say?" Was she trying to be smart? That was my initial thought but I didn't want to go there, so I spoke up a notch, "I need a rapid test". She smiled and said, "Okay, let me call the counselor and he'll be right up. Sign in and you can have a seat." I started to write my real name on the clip-board but then I realized that I didn't have to show

ID. This was a free confidential service, so I signed in as Jackie Scott.

As I sat with my head down, breezing through magazines that I had no interest in and trying to keep my nerves from jumping out my body, I heard this tall, slender white middle-aged male calling out for a patient and I put my head back into the publication. I wasn't reading any of the articles or looking at the ads; I was only trying to go unnoticed and I didn't want to make eye contact with anyone. Then it dawned on me, the male was calling my alias, Jackie Scott, and I needed to hurry up and acknowledge him before he went back into his office. I stood up and said, "Sorry, here I am." He smiled and said, "Right this way." He led me from the medium sized lobby into a narrow off-white hallway, and into an exam room. I was a ball of nerves and in the next twenty minutes I would find out if my life was over.

"Ms. Jackie, do you mind if I call you Jackie?"

"No, that's fine."

"Well, my name is John and I understand that you are here for a rapid HIV test. There's a standard one page form that I must go over with you before I begin. It explains the test and I'll ask you a few questions. When I'm done, I'll need you to sign the consent form. Alright?"

"That's fine." He pulled a form out of the top cabinet in the small examination room.

"Have you had unprotected sex with anyone in the past six months?"

"Yes, but only my husband?"

"Do you think he's infected?"

"No… but how can you really know?"

"You're right. The only way to know is by getting tested. Did you ever have sex with a same sex partner?"

"No!"
"Please don't take offense, these are just standard questions. We don't know unless we ask."
"Okay."
"Do you use any drugs, which would involve sharing needles?"
"No, do I look like a drug addict!"
"No...Jackie, remember these questions are standard and not meant to offend you."
"I'm sorry I'm just not use to this...but I'm okay. Just go ahead."
"If you were to have a positive result, do you think you'd harm yourself?"
"I don't want to think like that, I just need to know."
"No problem. Print your name and address at the bottom of the form and sign and date it."

I started writing my real name but quickly scratched it out once I realized my error. Then I wrote my alias in but had to take a few minutes to come up with a phony address. At first I couldn't think of any streets. But then I wrote in 1258 Chestnut Street because when I almost hit a biker trying to get to the clinic, the last thing I remembered was that address as the rider rode past with her middle finger high up in the air. I didn't know if he'd check it out but I wasn't giving up my real information.

"Okay Jackie, now I'm going to start the test. What I need you to do is thoroughly rub this swab along the top and bottom of your gums. You don't have to do it too hard, just make sure you firmly rub it on your gum-line." The swab looked like a shorter version of a pregnancy test, with a thicker applicator stick. The results read the same way, one line for no HIV and two lines if you're dead. I rigidly rubbed the test swab against my gums because I wanted the test to be accurate and I didn't want to take a re-test. After I swabbed my gums, I placed the test applicator into this small clear container, which was the same size as the cup they used for urine samples. Then he turned the test away from me. This really upset me because these were my results, why should they face him? Instead of sitting and wondering why, I asked.

"Why can't I watch the results?"

"It's just another standard. We give patients the choice to sit in the waiting room for twenty minutes or they can wait in the room with us, but we have to be the first to see their results."

That wasn't the answer I wanted. I wanted to watch each grueling moment to see if I be picking out a casket for me and Charles, or if he was going to get a solo urn because I was ready to set fire to his ass for giving me Chlamydia. But no matter how much I fussed and complained with John he wouldn't turn the test around. He tried to make small talk about the great weather we were having and how quickly the day was passing, but I wasn't in the mood. I decided to sit in silence while my brain ate away at my thoughts. If only the rapid test could have been instantaneous like a pregnancy test. Instead this twenty minute torture was my final thought before hearing my name called.

"Okay Kendra you had a non-reactive test."

"What?" I sat on the edge of my seat unsure of the terminology.

"You're not infected." The results lifted the weight of the world off my shoulders. I sighed with relief as he gave me more information.

"Listen, I know you're negative but its best if your partner gets tested. It's very possible that he could be infected even if you are not. Also if this is a recent infection you may have to get re-tested because it can take up to six months for HIV to be recognized in your body."

So all the premature good feelings I had felt evaporated because I still wasn't out of the woods. I immediately asked him if I could have a moment to myself and he stepped out of the room while I called Charles.

"Hi Baby, where you at?"

"I'm sitting in an HIV clinic and you need to get down here!"

"What!"

"Charles you gave me Chlamydia and I came down here to make sure that's all you gave me…Right now I don't want to talk about anything, I just want you to come here and get tested!"

"Baby…"

"No Charles, just get here. Don't bring my girls…are you home?"

"Yes." He said in a dazed tone.

"Good. I sent a text to Keyona and she'll be there in five minutes. Hurry up and get here because they close at four."

Charles was silent and took a few moments before agreeing to come to the center. It was almost three twenty and I knew it would take him at least fifteen to twenty minutes to get to the center. When John walked back into the room I asked him if Charles could be tested today, and he said, "If he's on his way he'll get tested today." Thankfully in addition to being one of the counselors, he was also the manager and responsible for closing this branch.

At three-fifty-two, John was called to the front desk over the loud speaker for a patient check-in, and I knew it was Charles. When he entered the room his eyes were flooded with shame and guilt. He held his head down and sat in the chair next to mine, as John began introducing himself and explaining the testing process. Looking at him disgusted me and he no longer was he the strong, picture perfect man I had fallen in love with. Currently he was nothing more than a piece of shit that had ruined my home, my life…and our future. When John began asking him questions about his recent sexual activity, I tuned in and I waited to hear his response. "Have you had sex with anyone new in the past six months?" Charles looked at me and a tear rolled down his eye as he responded, "Yes…with my ex-wife."

I didn't understand, he had just admitted to sleeping with his ex, a woman he claims wasn't the one for him. After he had promised to be faithful to me, after he had listened to me share my fears on infidelity, and after he had promised to protect me and my heart from any harm. He pledged to take care of me and my girls physically, financially, and emotionally for the rest of our lives. The energy in the room had turned hostile and without warning I reached over and slapped the saliva out of Charles's mouth. John jumped up and asked me to leave the room, but Charles told him it was okay and I could stay. I wasn't going anywhere. This was my cheating ass husband and right now he was lucky that I wasn't taking a knife to his jugular or slamming my chair into his head and crushing his skull. The betrayal I felt was inconceivable. I had been nothing but honest, loving and faithful, and my rage was building.

John asked if I could maintain my cool while he began the test and I assured him I would. I was grateful that he wasn't complaining about it being ten after four, and what I needed to know now was Charles' results. Charles was a lair. Sweeping me off my feet just to drop me on my ass. Why did he go back to his ex? For all that he could have stayed with her. But what were the ties; they had no children, and shared no property. "Why the hell did you go back to her", I shouted as I began to stand closer to him. I felt like punching him but I just wanted answers. John was getting paranoid and he asked me if I'd stand in the hallway until he finished the test. But that wasn't going to happen. I wanted to be in the room when the results were read and John didn't have to worry about calling the cops until after he read them.

So I walked to the door and told John I'd keep my distance for now. He asked Charles to sign the consent form and I watched as he began to swab his gums. Charles knew not to list my address or his real last name because I had sent him a text, along with my alias when he was on his way to the center. When he signed the forms I couldn't believe what was happening here. I was going insane and it felt as if I was having an out-of-body experience. What would I do if Charles' results were positive, how would people treat me, would I be able to live with this virus, how long would I have to live, would I be sickly looking, coughing, skinny and frail, and dark? Charles was silent as I stood looking at John and the back of his test. Rapid wasn't rapid enough, and the twenty minute wait was going to cause me to have a stroke or massive heart attack.

"Charles, your test is non-reactive." The room was filled with sighs of relief.

"Thank God, Thank God", I repeated as Charles walked up to me and tried to hug me. Immediately I pushed him out of my way, and began thanking John for allowing us to stay after center hours. It was now four forty five and all I wanted to do was see my girls. I was okay! I was HIV negative and I could feel air once again flowing through my lungs.

John walked us to the door and unlocked the side glass exit door, and I thanked him one last time. He had been a saint in my time of need and I'd be forever grateful. As I walked to my car Charles needlessly followed me. I was done with him and his pleading couldn't penetrate me. It was all falling on deaf ears but he tried his best to tell me how sorry he was.

"Kendra, baby, I promise I'll make this up to you. I'm sorry."

"Charles you could never make this up to me! You wanted to play a game…well I hope you enjoyed it. I sure as hell didn't have any fun. You could have killed me you fucking idiot! Was she worth it…Was she!"

He couldn't say anything else. Now wasn't the time to talk because his actions had spoken volumes and I knew how much he loved me…Enough to put my damn life at risk!!!

Forgive or Let Go?
Chapter 5

Since school was out my mom agreed to take the girls for me until I felt better. She knew something was really bothering me, but she didn't pry, and for a week I sat in my bedroom crying and feeling like shit. I wasn't HIV positive but I had lost the man I loved. I knew it wasn't my fault but I kept questioning why he had cheated. I wanted to know what I wasn't doing to make him happy. I wasn't some bum chick trying to use him, I had my own. I got up every day and made money, I kept a clean house, my girls weren't rude and bratty, and they were really great kids. Was it the sex, I questioned. Yet I knew it couldn't have been because it was always great…so what was I missing? I should have hated the ground he walked on but he was a part of my soul. Every moment was about him and I couldn't fake it, even though I was trying. I broke our picture frames, burned a few of our photos, and I even buried our marriage certificate in the backyard.

Every time Charles called I wouldn't pick up and it was unexplainable how seeing his name on the Caller-ID brought me comfort, yet pain at the same time. A few times he showed up at the house but he never used his key to enter. I think he knew I wasn't ready to deal with seeing him. I had so many questions but I knew I wasn't ready for the answers. Even more I couldn't look at him knowing what I felt was mine, what we had, was nothing more than an everyday special and he had not only shared our love but had done it without protection.

By the end of the week I decided to reach out to Toni. I hadn't talked to her since our fight and because of our last conversation I didn't bother inviting her to my wedding nor did she bother to show up. I knew it wouldn't be the most peaceful reunion but right now I needed her and she's never let me down when I really, truly needed her.

"So who died?"

"Nobody Toni, how are you?"

"I'm fine but I'm not sure why you're calling me." I began to tear up but did my best to hold them in.

"I just wanted to see how you were doing."

"Bullshit. My life has been doing just fine and from what I hear, so has yours. I terminated you from my life and it serves you no purpose to call, so don't!"

"Toni, please don't start …I need you!"

I started to let all the tears fall and began telling her about my ordeal and how I felt so alone. After I finished giving her the painful details about what had went down, I wasn't sure how Toni would respond. I apologized to her for all I had done and said, then asked her if I could come to Raleigh and spend some time with her, until I got my mind together.

"Kendra no matter what happens with us; you'll always be my cousin. If you need to come down, get here and I'll be here for you. Do you need me to come up and get you?"

"No…I wouldn't inconvenience you like that."

"Now come on now, didn't I offer?"

"Yes."

"Well you ain't inconveniencing me!"

"Toni its okay, the ride will do me some good. I'm going to leave in the morning and I'll call you before I come."

"Make sure you pack your earpiece cause I'll talk to you on the ride down…if you need someone to talk to."

"You're right about that…Well I'm going to take a nap and then get myself ready. I'll see you tomorrow and thanks again.
"No problem, I love you Kendra."
"Love you too, bye."

Immediately I called my job and told my supervisor I'd be out on Family Medical Leave (FMLA) for another week. The time I had saved for Disney World was out the door, the trip was over and so was my marriage. The next morning, I began gathering my clothes and as I was looking for my ear-piece the phone rang. I thought it was Toni but it ended up being Charles. I didn't answer so he started texting me, pleading with me to pick up the phone. I ignored him and he began calling the house phone. I was tempted to pick up but why would I? There were no words that he could speak to ease my pain. And even though I couldn't hide the way I truly felt about him, because the love I had for him was something I wanted the world to know, I just didn't know how to move past this mess. So I continued gathering my things until I saw his text saying if I didn't pick up the phone, he was coming over and this time he'd use his key.

I knew I wouldn't pick up but I didn't know how I'd react if he came into the house. So when I heard the door open, I stopped gathering my things and sat on the bed until he came upstairs.
"Where are you going Baby?"
"Charles I don't owe you any explanations?"
"What, I'm your husband."
"Were you my husband when you were fucking that bitch?" I asked.
He didn't respond.

"That's exactly what I thought. Charles we don't have anything together. We don't have any children together and I'm not pregnant, and we won't be having any…so what do you want?"
"Kendra I love…"
"Shut up Charles…that's the last thing I want to hear!"
"Okay Kendra, tell me what I can do, what I have to say. I'm lost without you…I need my family, I need my wife!"
"Charles, tell me the truth. That's it…why would you go to her…what did I do, what wasn't I doing!"
"No Baby, it wasn't anything you didn't do. I made a foolish mistake. I really fucked up!"
"Why Charles…what does she have that I don't?"
"The truth is I never got closure from our relationship. She was the first woman who made me feel like a man and I was madly in love with her. She left me and that's why we broke up, so I was never able to get closure."
"So what was I, a fucking fill in until the closer came back?!"
"No, that's not what I'm saying. What I'm saying is I'm just trying to keep it real with you. Enough lies, I've done enough damage. I just want you to hear me out."
"Charles do you still love her?"
"…No, I don't."
"Well why did you have to think about it?"
"I didn't have to think about it, I wanted to tell you that I loved you but I knew you didn't want to hear it."
"You take me for some type of fool, don't you?"
"Baby, never. I don't and won't ever hurt you again if you give me another try…I promise you!"
"Your words are as dependable as my eggs right now, they just can't be trusted and I don't know when or if that day will come!"

"Kendra don't worry about the baby, if you don't want to have our child…if that's the pain I have to bear, I'll do that."
"Oh don't you worry. You are never going to lay with me again, let alone taste me. She's here for that."
"Kendra, don't do this to us, don't…You know you love me. I know I messed up but I see now it wasn't worth it."
"Yes you see now, after I just finished swallowing a daily dose of horse pills for you and your ex-wife's infections!!!"
"All I'm asking you to do is please give me another chance. Let me man up for my mistakes and make things better. If you just give me a chance, I'm going to do everything to strengthen our family."
"Charles I'm the strength of my family! I'm the only one my girls and I can depend on and you're no longer welcomed in my home! When I'm gone, make sure you take all of your shit and every reminder that you ever stayed here."
"Kendra you don't mean that…you're just hurt right now."
"Charles, walk me to the bathroom."
"Sure. What's the matter?"
"Nothing, I just want you to walk me."

As he followed behind me, he put his hands on my shoulders and kept apologizing. When we were inside, I walked over to the toilet and lifted up the toilet seat. Then I flung my wedding ring into the toilet bowl. He rushed over to get the ring out but I flushed it before he had a chance to reach the toilet. Our toilet flushed with commercial strength, so he really had no chance once I pulled the toilet handle.

He sat on the floor in disbelief shaking his head and sobbing, as I walked out the door and began to take my suitcases downstairs. I didn't want to see him anymore. I had never given this man any reason to hurt me. There was always one thing I asked him not to do, and that was play with our love. I was faithful, not only physically but my mind was his. Each molecule of my body belonged to Charles and the thought of him fornicating was never my fear, I thought I had found perfection. But how perfect can a man be? He's made of weak flesh and too often he allows the little brain to override the common sense of the big one.

In a last attempt to keep me from leaving he said, "Kendra, I'll do anything, just don't leave me." That was easy; I wouldn't make it too hard for Charles. I asked him to give me one reason why I should stay, as the lyrics from a Tracy Chapman song played in my head. If he could come up with just one good reason I would put my bags down and work things out…he couldn't.

Momentary Escape
Chapter 6

The five hour drive to Raleigh was tortuous. It was a mental catastrophe and as much as I tried to concentrate on the road and take in the scenery, I just couldn't ignore my feelings of betrayal and the pain that burned deep in my soul. My mind couldn't shut down and I tried to listen to my music but when '*You Complete Me*' played from my Kelly Price CD, I was close to having a nervous breakdown. Mentally I tried to replay each moment of our short marriage to see if I had missed something. Charles was never distant with his love and never came home late. He hadn't done anything out of the ordinary but he found time to step out on me. '*Healing For My Soul'* crept up on me and the lyrics were what I needed. '*I need a healing for my soul, please Lord a healing for my soul'*. I cried out while gasping for air. I couldn't breathe and my chest felt heavy. Every song reminded me of how much I loved Charles but also recapped his cheating. I had enough of the musical emotional rollercoaster, so I cut the damn radio off and continued my drive with my faucet dripping of tears.

As soon as I entered the city, at six in the evening, I called Toni on my cell. It would only take fifteen minutes more for me to get to her and I wanted her to meet me outside the apartment complex. When I pulled up she opened my door and said, "Get out cousin". When I stood up she hugged me and said, "We are family first. I love you and you're gonna be okay." I needed to hear that because I sure as hell didn't feel okay, not for one minute. But right now I needed to make a run to the liquor store and rack up on the antidote for a broken heart. Although I knew it wouldn't be a permanent healing, I just needed enough margaritas to get me through the night.

When we got back from the Wine & Spirits, Toni helped me with the bags and I quickly made it to her second floor apartment. Toni's place was a complete replica of an IKEA's floor model; with warm earth tones throughout. Everything was in its place but you could tell she was a party girl by the amount of liquor on the shelf, oh and the stripper pole she had mounted in her dining room.

She only had one bedroom but it was very spacious. She began to make our first batch of drinks and she made me smile when she said "Sugar rim, no salt for Kendra". I sat on the floor and lay on my back. I felt a few tears escape but Toni wasn't having it. She ran over with my first drink -a strawberry margarita-cut on her Bose System and began blasting party music. "Get cha ass up and dance" Toni yelled out, as she grabbed me off the floor, almost spilling my drink. We started laughing and dancing around like wild girls and I was in need of every minute of it.

Three drinks in and I was well medicated. Toni always had to take things a step further, so she pulled out some weed and began rolling a blunt before going out on the balcony to smoke. I hadn't smoked weed since we were in high school-and I wouldn't call taking a few puffs of a joint really smoking- but tonight I was down, so I went out there with her. My first puff was a quick reminder that I was a newbie and the harsh cough behind it was soothed with a decent swallow of my new favorite drink, mango margarita. I smoked about half of the blunt with her before realizing I needed to sit my butt down and regroup, and then I made my way into the living room and found a comfortable spot on the coach.

Toni finished the blunt off then she came in an asked, “How you doin?” This was a very different Toni. The tone of her voice was very caring and she sounded genuinely concerned about me, instead of the cold, harsh, attacking bitch I had come to detest; and I was more than grateful for her compassion. Maybe she sympathized with me because Toni never had good luck with men. She was always chasing men and asking her friends and family to hook her up with a good guy. Before we stopped speaking I can’t remember a day that went by without her saying, “I want a man”. I didn’t know what to do for her because with all her shit, I didn’t think there was a man out there that could handle my crazy cousin. On the outside Toni’s got it going on. She has a beautiful light butter-toffee complexion, slender built model type body with long legs, and the perfect shaped face for the short-cuts she wears. Toni’s celebrity look-a-like would definitely be Toni Braxton, but personality wise she can be compared to the psychotic ladies who played in Misery or Sybil. I think if she can get the emotionally unstable, Bi-polar/Schizophrenia division of herself together, she might actually have a chance with a man that’s out on the streets.

Toni’s been in a long term relationship with a guy named Rasool for the past six years, and he has fifteen years left to serve in a State penitentiary. She only knew him for two months before he got sentenced and she’s been visiting him and writing him ever since he went in for attempted murder and kidnapping. One moment she’s so in love and happy with her boo and the next she’s searching for a man on the outside.

Everybody thought she had lost her mind when she converted from Christianity to Islam for this guy. Rasool had bought and sent her a Quran but she didn't have a clue how to read the thing, so she bought the book 'The Quran for Dummies' to help her gain an understanding. Toni didn't take her time to learn much but she decided instantly to garb up from head to toe-face guard and gloves-and went to the Masjid with the sisters. She even had the nerve to tell her family she wouldn't be able to talk to us much because we weren't following the path that Allah had set for us. Yeah this new way of life all happened during the winter because as soon as summer broke she came out of those over-garments and went back to partying, drinking and smoking her weed. All of a sudden it became too hot for her to be a Muslim and every time I turned around she was saying "I swear to God" and "I'm truly blessed". I felt like she was truly touched because she had quickly reverted back to Christianity and when I first saw her out of her garments I had to say "Astaghfirullah". I had heard the girl run the damn saying in the hole once she took her Shahadah, and when I asked her what it meant she didn't know. It wasn't until I asked a male co-worker who practiced and actually respected Islam the meaning that we both discovered it meant- I ask Allah's forgiveness. I wondered if she even knew what it meant to take the Shahadah or what the Arabic words she said translated to in English, but Toni was caught up in Rasool that I'm sure she was simply following the leader because the act didn't last.

I personally believed a relationship with an inmate-who's locked up with no other woman to mess around with, who counts the days until your next visit, and dissects and cherishes each letter you write would be uneventful, but not when Toni's involved. That girl had more drama with Rasool than I'd had with someone who was free. She's already been banned from two institutions after getting busted for having sex with him in the visiting room by the snack machines. And since he's been in this new facility SCI Dallas, which is in Dallas, PA, she found another way to have sex with him without getting caught.

During the summer they have their family picnics and you're allowed to have more physical contact, which includes sitting on their laps, and you can stay inside the visiting room or go outside in their designated areas. She uses this time to celebrate Halloween early because she goes in her bag and pulls out the over-garments. She leaves the panties at home- for easy access of course- and she wears a thin slip under her top garment. She sits on this man's lap, surrounded by guards, inmates, visitors-women, men and children alike, and slowly rotates his dick as he struggles to maintain himself before busting inside of her. She then uses the thin slip beneath the over-garment as a rag to wipe of his and her cum. A bit confusing, I know, I was puzzled at first. These fools fuck in public and they're not alone. Toni has a few female friends who are also using the Muslim gear to get them some during the picnics, and they've got each other's back. They go as far as to watch out for the guards and have a code-word they use to alert each other. When they hear the word Quran they laugh and appear cheerful as if they are following picnic visitor-rules protocol in front of the passing guards. Crazy, I know but that's Toni. Not to mention the girl has been pregnant by him at least two times that I know of but she decided to terminate both pregnancies because as she stated "What I look like having his baby and he ain't even close to getting out."

I thought after hearing she had sex with this man in jail I had heard it all but she wasn't done shocking the hell out of me. I remember when Rasool called my phone and asked me how Toni was doing. At first I was dumbfounded because I had never spoken to this dude and he was all comfortable with me like we were family. Then I wondered why he was calling me asking about Toni. I knew I had to keep my mouth shut and listen up for clues. Rasool starts crying and said "I don't understand why she keeps miscarrying and now when she finally makes it full term the baby didn't survive?" Was he asking me a question because I knew Toni didn't lose any babies, and she sure as hell didn't carry no baby full term and have a stillborn, but what did he want me to say? Then he said "Man I got the pictures of our baby and this shit is just horrible. I don't know what I've done but Allah knows how badly I wanted my boy!" The lies she tells are a mess and the length she goes to prove this bull is even worse.

Toni went to this website called 'Missing Angels', where parents of stillborns post images of their deceased babies. There you can list information such as their names; birthdates, death date, and they also share their feelings about their loss with other parents. She got herself a picture of a black baby boy, and he looked like a sleeping angel who was swaddled in a blue blanket with little puppies running all over it, and the rest is history. I felt bad for him and sick to my stomach, and I didn't want to pretend any of this was true because I didn't want to have a permanent residence in hell, so I kept quiet. I wondered who could and would do this shit…only my cousin.

Now we were sitting on the floor talking about my husband and my pain-perfect counselor I know, but underneath all her drama was someone who had the ability to listen and speak encouraging and uplifting words that made me feel better. I was totally lifted and the vibrations of my cell quickly reminded me I forgot to call the girls. When I looked at my phone Charles had called me ten times and I had six new voice messages. I hurried and called my mom and she said the girls were just fine, and then I noticed Charles was calling on my other line. I decided to get off the phone with my mom and answer, but he began questioning me -asking what I was doing and who I was doing it with- as if he had any right. I quickly ended the interrogation with Charles, and Toni and I stayed up late until I dosed off.

Around nine in the morning, I got up and started to make breakfast. I made French toast, beef bacon, and cheese eggs. It was Saturday and Toni was off from work. She works for the water department, in the phone unit, and they don't work weekends. Instead of waking Toni up I put her plate in the microwave and sat on the couch and watched a little TV. Not even fifteen minutes into the morning show, and Charles was calling.

"Charles I don't want to talk to you… I will, but not right now."

"Listen, now is the time we need to talk. I need my wife back!"

"Charles why couldn't I be your wife when you slept with her…That was the time I wanted to be Mrs. Richardson!"

"I messed up baby, big time…but if you just let me explain why I did it."

"You really think that's gonna make it better…then go ahead!"

"Before I met you I was obsessed with that woman. From the way she touched me, talked to me…it was just me and her. Then she cheated on me and I couldn't forgive her..."

"And now you want me to forgive you?"

"Baby, please just listen. I did my best to put her out of my mind but I never got closure. But when I met you I felt all this was behind me..."

"Well obviously it's not! Charles you lied to me and you led me on. You could have told me about her. You didn't have to use me like some rebound chick."

"You not no damn rebound, you're my wife!"

"You told me that I was the missing part of your heart…but I see you got a big ass heart, and I don't know how many pieces you done lent the fuck out! In our home there were two addicts. I was hooked to Depo and you were craving your fucking ex-wife! Charles don't call me back today…right now I have to take some time for me!"

Let's Get This Party Started Right
Chapter 7

Charles needed to give it a rest. It was around one in the morning, and I had been sleeping on the couch until my mind realized my damn phone wouldn't stop vibrating. In our last conversation he had told me more than I wanted or needed to know, and now I wasn't in the mood for him calling me from an anonymous phone number.

"What Charles…I asked you to leave me alone!"

"This ain't Charles" she said, as I became instantly agitated because who the hell was this woman calling from an undisclosed number at one in the morning.

"Well who is this?" I demanded, as my exhausted voice now gained strength.

"It's Dana…"

"Okay Dana, it's clear you've got the right number because you would have said otherwise by now, so what do you want?"

"I'm trying to let you know about your so called husband…are you ready to hear the truth about him?" she asked, as I envisioned a pleased grin appearing on her face.

"The truth…the truth is that anything you have to tell me, I already know and I'm not sure why you feel it's your duty to notify me about mine…because you're his ex, so try your best to move on."

"His ex…" she said, in a sarcastic tone.

"Yeah you dirty bitch! Do yourself a favor and don't bother calling me with this dumb shit!" I screamed into the phone as this fool on the other end began to laugh.

"Firstly I ain't dirty, I'm delicious! And that's why he won't ever be yours. The papers may say ex but I'm always his first choice. By the way did you like your wedding gift?"
"What?!?!"
"And since I didn't get a chance to meet you at the church I just wanted to tell you the ceremony was beautiful."
"Listen bitch, I think it's best if you keep your infected ass away from me and my husband!" I hung up my cell phone as if I was slamming the handle of my house phone.

Charles didn't pick up his phone as I continued to call him for answers. I know this Dana wasn't at my wedding and if the gift she was talking about was that nasty woman's disease- Chlamydia, she was truly a trifling, disrespectful bitch. Our ceremony was only supposed to be filled with our family and a small selection of our friends. Was he stupid enough to invite her? Was she really there? I wanted answers immediately but he wouldn't pick up his damn phone. Now I was ready to race home. I had a bit of a hangover and my head was spinning, but now that I couldn't find out if she was a vicious liar, my headache been upgraded to a migraine. I thought about waking up Toni but she was snoring so loudly, I didn't want to interrupt anyone who was lucky enough to get that kind of good sleep.

As badly as I wanted to get him on the phone I couldn't, so I did the next best thing. I started texting him, telling him I wanted a divorce, then I asked if his ex was at our wedding and more importantly I asked how she got my number. We didn't have any mutual friends because my circle was so tight; it was damn near invisible; so it was no way she got my number from someone I knew. He must have dosed off after he slept with her and then she went through his cellphone and got my number- that had to be it. I begin analyzing and over-analyzing the situation. I was trying my best to wait for truthful answers but my patience didn't exist. She was flaunting this crap in my face and Charles was responsible for this entire mess. I kept calling and texting Charles until he called me back around three am, and as soon as I heard his voice I began.

"Dana called me Charles…You invited that bitch to our wedding though!"

"Kendra, no, calm down. What are you talking about?"

"Okay, so you want to play that game. I'm talking about why she just called me bragging about giving me Chlamydia and being at our wedding!" I paused and waited for his delayed response.

"Kendra she's lying… she wasn't there. She's just upset because I told her I can't deal with her on any level. I let her know it's really over and she's trying to to make you mad." He pleaded.

"Oh you did, well did you let her know my phone number too?"

"No baby, I don't know how she got your number, but I damn sure didn't give it to her."

"Maybe she went through your phone while you were over there fucking her brains out!"

"Kendra, don't let her stand in the way of our happiness…"

"Our happiness!!! You're the one who ruined that for me!"

I hung up the phone and he kept calling, but I didn't want to hear it anymore. Before his ex called I was contemplating going home and trying to work on rebuilding our crumbled relationship. I didn't want to lose him but now I wasn't sure why I cared. After sitting on the balcony for a while and enjoying the cool early summer morning breeze, I went back onto the couch and lay down.

Later that day I went out to lunch with Toni and her friends, Masood and Eric. We meet up at Globe-an Italian- American restaurant at seven o'clock in downtown Raleigh. Initially I didn't want to go because it seemed like a double date, but after the phone call I wasn't about to sit in the house and mope.

Masood was Toni's boo of the week and I could see why. He was a Muslim-brother with a beard that was longer than Moses. I seriously doubted if she knew anything about him because when it came to dark-skinned men with those beards, all her commonsense went out the window. It was like she was obsessed with those beards and pertinent information, like full name, age, occupation, number of children; previous arrest, education background, and current address all seemed secondary. But to be fair, he wasn't a bad looking brother and Eric, a tall light bright, wasn't my type but I was out and about to mask my pain and force myself to have a good time.

Eric and I sat on the same side, across from Toni and her friend and the conversation was light and fun. Masood had a great sense of humor and made me laugh until my stomach hurt, and Eric had some good follow-ups. We were all having a few drinks. I was back on my margarita kick and enjoyed two key-limes. Eric started getting kind of close and wanted to know more about me than I wanted to share. Then he asked, "Oh so you're married" as he looked at my left hand. My silly butt said, "No" because I wasn't wearing a ring but they knew I was lying when he said, "So why Toni tell us you were married." I was busted and wanted to pop her in her big mouth, so I replied, "I was married but we're separated and will soon be divorced." Eric didn't seem to buy my story, as he sarcastically giggled at my response. But I didn't care because I was going home in a week and there was no harm in having dinner with an okay looking man, and thanks to the alcohol I was feeling a little frisky.

Toni invited the fellas back to her apartment and with the drinks talking to and for me, I wasn't against it. When we got back to her place she put on some DC go-go music and led Masood into the dining room to work out the pole. This girl was a hot mess, acting like a damn stripper and if we were at a booty-bar I wouldn't have been able to tell her apart from the working girls. But after a few more drinks I was right in there with her doing the booty clap. Eric was all over me and my nipples hardened as he gently passed my blouse and placed a few dollars in my bra. I was enjoying myself and when Toni and Masood went into her bedroom, I knew they were about to enjoy themselves as well.

As Eric and I sat on the couch, he began rubbing my shoulders and started talking to me in this very sexy voice. I thought it was cute and as soon as I started getting in the grove of the hilarious but fulfilling lap dance he was giving me, my phone rang. It was the anonymous number again and when I picked up I wasn't surprised that it was Dana. I excused myself and walked out onto the balcony to talk to her. "What now…are you calling for Charles?" I asked, as she laughed and replied, "I got him already, I just called to see how you were doing?" She had to be joking because there was no way adult women act like this. I wanted to snatch her through my phone and show her how I was doing. I was getting upset but I know that's what she wanted. She wanted to get a rise out of me and she was, but I had to contain myself. "Dana if you want to find out how Charles is doing or where he is you don't have to go through me to get him…or do you? Calling me ain't gonna bring you no closer to him. So stop calling me and go get your man, I'm busy."

I silenced my ringer and went back on the couch with Eric. It was my turn he said so I started to give him a lap dance. While my hips moved and my ass shook, my clothing began to disappear. As I faced him, his firm, smooth hands began caressing my neck and slid down to my breast. Slowly placing my nipple into his mouth, he began twirling his tongue around my areola. When he tossed me over onto my back the show of force turned me on, and I didn't stop him when I saw him unfastening his pants. I didn't know much about Eric and I didn't want to know about him. If he had a girlfriend or a wife, I didn't care because I saw how unimportant that was in my own situation. None of that mattered to me as he slid inside of my watering garden hole. All I wanted was to get it and throw it back, to show just how I was feeling on the inside-fucked.

The week of partying with Eric at Toni's house went by quickly. Toni and I stayed up all hours of the night, and during the week we had so much we wanted to do that she called out twice from her job. We were drinking on and off (mostly on), and although Eric and I were sleeping with each other most of the week, midweek Toni had swapped out Masood for another dark-skinned bearded Muslim, named Elijah. Toni's apartment had turned into a twenty-four hour party house and the alcohol and weed was endless.

During my last night at the apartment Toni and Elijah had taken the party to another level when they started doing lines of coke. Toni rolled up a dollar bill into a makeshift straw faster than my eyes could process her paper talents. I was shocked to see her going in like a professional and once we made eye contact she knew I was a bit thrown off by her new hobby. She pulled me into her bedroom to tell me it was something she did occasionally, but I wasn't sold. She was snorting those lines down too casually and Toni's always been the type to try and use anything. She had offered me ecstasy the third day I was there, and what did I do, I tried it. I was up all night and most of that night is a blur. But I wasn't judging, it just wasn't my thing and luckily for the both of us we didn't have addictive personalities-well not to drugs at least.

When it was time for me to head home I knew I had to get back to reality. No longer could I ignore it. I loved Charles and what I wanted most was to be with my family. Truth be told I felt vindicated for enjoying myself with Eric, but now he was a thing of my past and there would be no further contact. Toni didn't want me to go but that girl was too much for me. My cousin was a wild-child and I'd never be able to keep up with her. We had two different types of lifestyles and energy levels. All I wanted now was to work things out with my husband and see how we could clean up this mess.

Back To Reality
Chapter 8

After two months of constant arguing, sexual frustrations, and dealing with trust issues, we both agreed we needed professional help if our marriage was going to last.

Dr. Vincent Calloway had a couples counseling practice on the 1900 block of N 63rd Street which was not too far from our house. So thanks to my mother's suggestion, we made an appointment. The office was warm, all neutral colors with beautiful deep oak colored hardwood floors. He sat behind a cherry oak desk with a Mac-book on top, as we sat on a comfortable couch just a few feet away. There was a TV and DVD player in the room that made me wonder if we had to watch a video. He also had a white board in the room with a sign that said 'Take Notes', which he used to make notes should we need to write anything down. As beautiful as the room was, it was still very uncomfortable considering the circumstances and my nerves were jumping.

Our first visit started off with introductions. Dr. Calloway, a tall, dark, and handsome, distinguished looking man, who seemed like he would never age past thirty-five was fifty-seven, with five beautiful daughters and he'd been married for twenty-two years. Faithfully married he added. After giving us some personal background information on him, he told us about his scholastic and time-in qualifications; which seemed unnecessary because I was ready to get right to the purpose of this visit; Charles's cheating. I didn't care what schools he went to or how long he had worked in his field, I only wanted to know if it was a way to fix our marriage. Getting to know each other only took time away from our one hour session and I wanted to fix this all in that short time. Even though mentally I knew that wasn't possible I stayed hopeful.

So with the formalities out of the way, he asked "What brings you two here today?" On the couch I was sitting a few inches away from Charles, but I didn't look at him before responding "My husband cheated on me with his ex-wife and he gave me Chlamydia." Now I'm sure the good doctor had heard plenty of people's personal stories but when I said Chlamydia his eyes almost popped out of his head. Charles started to interrupt me, but Dr. Calloway suggested he just listen and promised he'd have his turn when I was done.

When I finished explaining why I thought we were there, Dr. Calloway handed me some tissues because at this point reliving the memories of Charles and Dana sleeping together hurt like hell, so the tears had begun to fall. The thoughts of Charles touching her with the hands that he had promised belonged to me and the images of him gently and sensually kissing her lips were grueling and they made me sick. I wasn't embarrassed to tell him how hurt I was because I'm sure he could see it. Charles had pretended to be faithful and he had hurt meet deeply.

Dr. Calloway asked Charles to playback what he had heard me say and when he was done, I felt he had got it all wrong. Then he asked Charles, "Why are you here?" He immediately looked over at me and said "Because I fucked up" and I shouted "You damn right you did!" We had an exchange of you did me wrong and I'm sorry for a minute or two, before Dr. Calloway stopped writing on his Mac-book and intervened.

"Kendra do you want to work this out?" he asked, looking into my eyes as if he already knew the answer.
"Yes…but how can I trust him?"
"No, I didn't ask if you trusted him, I asked if you want to work this out."
"Yes…I want to be with my husband."
"Charles, do you want to work this out?"
"Yes!"
"Can you make a commitment to yourself and promise to keep your pants up and focus your attention on your wife and rebuilding your family?" Dr. Calloway asked, even though it felt like he was giving out a direct order instead of asking a question.
"That's not a problem. That's all I want."

I jumped up from the couch because I didn't know if I could believe anything Charles promised. And why should I? I was out of my seat for a minute before Dr. Calloway walked over and asked me to take my seat back on the couch, but I shook my head no.

"Kendra let me tell you what I see here. There is a man who came into my office with his wife. He didn't make excuses for what he did. He listened to you and heard the pain he has caused you. He spoke of you two as a unit, and wants to rebuild what he has broken. Let me tell you something…I've worked in cooperate offices and for the last ten years I've been in private practice, and I rarely see African American males in either environment. Our people often look down on counseling and believe only crazy folks sit on the couch but I'd be the first to tell them that's a lie. I get a little treatment here and there myself. And as a man, see we are different than our counterparts. We foolishly let the little head get us into trouble because we need to work on strengthening our will power and understand the loss ain't worth the momentary gain; however that doesn't make us all bad. This man here has said he's sorry and wants to work, and you can trust I'd never let a women sit up here and be played for a fool. I have too much respect for my wife, my mother and all my daughters to let that happen to you. If I thought it was a waste, I'd come out and tell both of you because I'm a straight shooter. I've done it plenty of times before because I'm all about healing and healthy relationships, not the drama. Are you guys willing to put in the work?"

"Yes." We said simultaneously.

"Okay here's your assignment for our next session."

I sat back on the couch and began to take the note that he had written on the white board. He wanted us to let go of the past, as much as we could, and make two lists. One for all the great and amazing things we loved about each other, and another for the things we disliked. When we came to the next appointment we would go over them. Our hour session had quickly turned into two, and we both walked out of Dr. Calloway's office feeling a bit of relief. I'll admit I felt there was some hope that I could eventually trust my husband again.

That night Charles asked if he could take me out to dinner, and after the girls came home from school Keyona came over to babysit. This was the first time we had been out together since I had come back from Toni's, and it was something I missed. I figured we grab a bite to eat from the Outback- which was now my favorite place to eat, thanks to their mouthwatering, tender lamb-chops. But Charles drove me to a drive-in movie theater in New Jersey. My initial thoughts were how cute and romantic, but they were soon followed by suspicion. I wondered if he had brought Dana here because I'd never been here... and what was his motive? I was treating him more like a stranger than someone who was out with her husband. I knew Dr. Calloway said if I wanted things to change, I had to be willing to forgive him and move on, but it was so difficult.

The blonde busty waitress looked silly when she awkwardly skated up to our car carrying a pen and a small note pad to take our order. We laughed because she was acting so dippy and it took her four times to get my order right. As we ate our cheeseburgers, fries and drank milkshakes, I loosened up. When I looked over at most of the cars in the drive-through, it was clear that this was make-out central. I felt like a school girl and it didn't take long before Charles and I joined the crowd. I missed touching his skin, tasting his lips, and the way he touched me made me tremble. My body belonged to him and when he touched me, it confirmed he was the ruler of my body. He started to nibble on my neck and then he actively began sucking my breast. He was like a starving baby who had yearned to feed from my nipples. He hadn't touched me in months and he was marking his territory. Now I was good and ready. He slowly slid his finger into my pussy and I could feel the crouch of my panties getting soaked. It had been too long and I needed him.

We quickly hoped over the front seats and got into the backseat, and then Charles took my jeans off. But when he tried to enter into me raw and uncut, I denied his access because the last thing I wanted was another STD. He pleaded with me and promised he was clean but that wasn't good enough. I wanted Charles and even though I craved him more than I could stand, my health was more important than a momentary fix. Charles was frustrated and said, "So what you want me to do? You think I'm going to put on a condom with my wife?" I looked at him and thought about what he had just said, and then replied "That wouldn't be a bad idea." He let out a burly sigh of aggravation and started to fasten up his pants, before getting out the back door and into the driver seat. I couldn't give two-shits about his little hissy-fit because it was me who had felt the poison of his previous actions. Lightening was not about to strike twice…not if I could help it.

On the ride home he didn't say much and it bothered me. Why he was acting as if things were supposed to be normal was beyond me. Now, yes we had one good counseling session and I said I would forgive, but forgiveness wasn't going to involve forgetting, and better yet all this wasn't going to happen in the same day. This was a work in progress and I just wasn't there yet. So if we had to ride in silence unto I got home, I would put up with that because I wasn't changing my mind about using protection.

Keyona was sleeping on the couch when we walked into the door and he briskly woke her up, paid her, and told her he would take her home. I went to the girl's bedroom and checked on them before showering and getting ready for bed. I heard Charles walk back into the house while I lay on the bed, and I continued reading my horoscope in the Philadelphia's Daily News Paper. I knew Keyona lived close by but he must have flown her home. My horoscope suggested forgiveness for an individual who had wronged me. I laughed and softly replied, "Yeah right." When Charles entered our bedroom he looked at me mysteriously, and then asked me if I had changed my mind. One of my pet peeves is repetition. If I said no, then don't ask me again. He knew how much this irritated me and when I ignored him, he decided to ask me again. So now I felt he deserved a dose of the silent treatment, but even though I wouldn't respond, he kept asking me. I reached over to my night stand and turned off the lamp. I'd rather him sit in the dark and talk to himself than to aggravate me.

He walked out of the room and got into the shower. I tried to fall asleep quickly because even though I wanted to make things right; I just didn't know how. When he got into the bed, he began to rub my back and his hands slid lower and lower, until it was clear he wasn't taking no for an answer. He kissed my body and although I tried to play sleep, when his tongue entered my forbidden garden, he knew I was fully awake. I grabbed his shoulders and tried to contain myself but he was too good at this. How this man's tongue had more power than a silver bullet amazed me. Then he made his way up to my lips and told me "Put it in!" I wouldn't and he said it again, but I wasn't going to. He got up and I heard him walk over to the dresser before getting back in the bed. "This is what you really want" he asked, while handing me a condom. I knew we had always had condoms in the house but they were for show because we never used them. But now as I tore the wrapper open and began to slide it on, I knew they would become a routine in our sexual relationship.

As he entered me I felt tears forming, and they began to softly fall down my face. I was so hurt and the idea of using protection with my husband didn't seem ideal. I wanted to feel my man…my chocolate Mr. Good-Bar and I wanted the sensation from every curve, and each vibration, and of course I longed for the pulse and jolt as he ejaculated deep inside of me Charles didn't even notice me crying, as he humped on me as a mammal in heat. The intimacy and trust we shared had been broken, and I thought sleeping with him might repair it but I was wrong. As he exhaled heavily upon me and let out this caged moan, while cuming inside his plastic partner, I wanted him to get off of me immediately. He rolled over and removed the package, tied it in a nice little bow, tossed it in the waste basket on his side of the bed, wiped himself with a wash cloth, and kissed me on the cheek before telling me he loved me, and then he fell asleep. I didn't feel any love. It felt more like he needed a body to bust a nut in and I was the lucky winner. I wanted to express my feelings but I didn't have anyone to talk to; Charles was rocked. So I shut down my system and lay motionless until I fell asleep.

For the next several weeks Charles and I didn't have sex and there was tension between us. We returned to Dr. Calloway's office numerous times and even though the good on my list outweighed the bad, I could not let go of his infidelity. Was I a bitter woman? I didn't know. I had never loved a man like I loved Charles and when you give your all, why shouldn't you get the same in return? I hadn't saved myself all those years for nothing, had I? These stereotypes and double standards are bullshit. I've heard so many women shouting "As long as he takes care of home, you got yourself a good man." I couldn't adapt to that, especially when I did a damn good job of that on my own. I had the same standards as my man. He didn't want a cheating whore so why would he think I did? Did he feel he could go out and sleep with some woman and come home to something wholesome? He was a damn fool. One thing I did get from my grandfather was his logic, because we both believed if you could do it, then why the hell can't I?

With no progress in our home I continued to make my bi-weekly weekend trips to Toni's and Charles couldn't stand it. Once at my mini-vacation spot I didn't bother calling him and I knew the girls were in good hands, so I had no worries. At Toni's I was able to feel free and our relationship had grown stronger. We were getting along perfectly and growing closer as each day passed. When I was there Eric was definitely a routine visitor and we did our thing here and there. I didn't feel any significant attachment to him, and at least when we fucked I didn't have any resentments or apprehensions.

As usual Toni had her beard of the week and she did a little recycling and made a few upgrades. She couldn't settle down and was having the time of her life. Each weekend I was there she'd tell me all about her escapades and which lover was the biggest and the best. I damn near peed on myself from laughing when she told me she had married some bearded dude and divorced him the next day. Luckily for her it was an Islamic ceremony. With no witnesses and nothing filed in City Hall, when she told the guy she had to divorce him because he didn't satisfy her, he took his bruised ego and left her alone.

One day out of my trip was exclusively for us. She would make my favorite margarita, sugar rimmed of course, and we'd dance to her party music and stay up all night talking. When she suggested I forgive Charles and take the condom off I tried to listen to her but listening was as far as it went. I just couldn't continue to sleep with him knowing he had slept with Dana no matter how many times we sat in Dr. Calloway's office.

I was really shocked at how mature and kind Toni was behaving and I wished she had been more like this when she was back at home. This was the bond that our mother's had wanted for us, and I was finally feeling like I had gained a sister and a best friend.

One Last Time!!!
Chapter 9

Charles wanted to know why it was so important for us to get tested again. So I explained to him it was the only way the condom would come off. After a year filled with counseling and protected sex, I wanted to be sure we were clean. By now, we had told John all about our situation and done away with our aliases, and we were back in his office for a third test. Originally I figured we should take the test every six months as long as we were together, but after this test I was done. I no longer enjoyed the feel of the plastic bag and it didn't matter how thin or sensitive the condom was, nothing was like the real deal. Being a family and a great wife to Charles were my biggest desires now, and I was going to cut down my bi-weekly weekends trips to Toni's. I actually visited Raleigh to spend girl's time with Toni because Eric had become nothing more than someone in the way. But now she'd have to come see me occasionally because I didn't want her to feel like I was cutting her off, but I'd definitely have to be home more often with Charles if I wanted our marriage to improve.

As John swabbed us and sat our applicators in their cups we causally sat and waited. We had become professional test takers and it was now a calm procedure that was filled with general chatter. John was a very cheerful man and I always complemented him on something, whether it was his hair, a watch, or his outfit. He loved compliments because he took pride in his appearance and he'd widely smile and said "thank you", flashing his pearly whites. Then we'd continue our small talk.

Twenty minutes breeze through like hurried wind when you're at ease, and as he turned to look at Charles' test he said "Everything's fine Charles, no worries." Charles smiled and looked at me and boldly said, "Of course not. I told my wife we didn't have to come here no more." He was excited because now he knew he no longer had to purchase condoms from Walgreens and Rite-aid. John then turned to my test but now he paused. It was that kind of moment when you knew nothing good was going to be said. Giving the results of a negative HIV test was easy, nothing to it; just let the patient know that he or she was fine and that they could go on living a safe, satisfied, healthy lifestyle. But there was this pause. I was looking for his eyes to get a reading but he hadn't looked back at me, or near my direction.

"John what's the matter?" I demanded.

"Well, Kendra don't be alarmed…we have false test results sometimes. I'm going to have to re-test you."

My heart dropped, no it blew the hell up in my chest cavity! I wanted to see the test so I grabbed it and at the sight of two lines I started screaming.

"Oh My God, Oh My God…No Charles, Oh My God!!!"

Charles grabbed me as if he was trying to stop me from losing my damn mind and said, "Baby calm down, he just said sometimes they get a false result. Listen John; take both of our tests over again!"

"No problem", he said as he pulled two new tests out of the drawer.

I sat in silence and this time twenty minutes, under duress, became the longest twenty minutes you'd never want to have in a lifetime. Each second felt as if it was driving deeper into my soul doing permanent damage. Charles kept rubbing my shoulders and the little examination room began to close in on me. The taste of panic overrode my taste-buds and I began to shake while my thoughts raced faster than the best NASCAR driver. What would I do if it was true, how long would I have to live, what would I do with my girls, how could this happen to me and why was Charles' test negative? I had been through this panic before and my world had been saved but now what were my results going to be?

"Kendra we're going to take a blood test… because…I'm so sorry this test is positive also." I listened as the words ripped my chest cavity apart and sucked the life out of my heart. I stared at the ground and I didn't feel clean enough to hold my head up and face my future. Charles, who a second ago was my rock and knew I was negative, was all tears and asked John, "Man, are you sure? How can my wife be positive when I'm negative?" John hesitated before answering. Then he said, "It's my responsibility to educate and provide my patients with life-sustaining treatment. We have to review the sexual history of your wife as well as any possible exposure to the virus since her last test. Kendra has there been any changes?" he said, and now he was looking for the answer in my eyes.

Charles became angry and shouted, "No she ain't been with no one, that's my wife man!" I could vaguely hear him because I was in another world. It was as if I was a lost soul spinning her heels and trying to find a place to sit still. What had I done? My head still hung to the floor and my body shook uncontrollably, like I was suffering from epilepsy. I wanted to talk but I couldn't. My brain wasn't sending the message to my vocal chords. I started sweating and then I felt chills and I still couldn't speak. John asked Charles to step out of the room for a minute so he could prepare my blood test. He was very hesitant because he didn't want to leave my side but eventually gave in to his request. When I reached for his hand, and said "It's alright." I was lying. Nothing was alright but I needed him to leave the room because I had a confession to make.

Toni's, my place of freedom and comfort had been just a bit too free. I used condoms with Eric but there had been several times when he had rubbed his bare penis against my raw vaginal opening; and there were the occasional slide-ins. I knew better than to sleep around without using protection, and I knew I didn't want anything brought home to me-which had already occurred-so how could I have been so sloppy! I was hurting and I didn't know how I could tell Charles but for now I had to come clean with John.

"John, I had a few encounters with a friend of mine but I never fully engaged…I let him slide it in a few times but other than that we always used a condom."

"Kendra, infected semen could have entered your body from him. Also how about oral or anal?"

"God I'm Going To Die!" I yelled, as John did his best to calm me.

"Did you engage in anal sex because that's the easiest way to pass the virus?"

"No we didn't do that or oral."

"Kendra, this isn't twenty years ago when everyone thought of this as a death sentence. There are people who go on living full and fulfilling lifestyles and never succumb to the virus."

"You think that'll be my outcome…"

"Kendra, everyone is different but let me get the blood sample and then we can talk more."

Now I watched him as he was more adamant about protecting himself because he reached for his gloves. Before, when he swabbed me, he hadn't used any but now he wasn't taking any chances. But who the hell could blame him. I was an infected woman whose life had just ended. Charles knocked on the door, then peered his head in and asked if I was okay. I'm sure he could see I wasn't anywhere close to being alright, but I tried my best to give him some comfort as I nodded yes. His eyes, which I quickly gazed upon, no longer had any white inside of them. The color had turned blood-shot red from all the crying he was doing in the hallway. If I was him, I would have run home, packed my shit, and left. He had no real ties to me and I'm sure he would have been granted a quick divorce under the circumstances. He wasn't poisoned and I felt guilty because I had put him in harm's way. I had made such a fuss about him sleeping with Dana, but at least he was smart enough to sleep with someone who only required a dose of pills to make it all go away.

Charles wasn't infected, so he didn't do this to me but Eric had. I wanted to leap down Raleigh and blow his fucking brains out, but for now it would be a week until my blood results came back before I could make any moves.

I was hurting and I sat in that chair and didn't flinch as John drew two tubes of blood from my left arm. As I stared at the contaminated blood, I couldn't see any difference in the color or in my physical appearance for that matter. I wasn't sick, hadn't lost weight, and didn't have any large marks, lesions, or degenerating wounds associated with HIV. But right

now I felt like I was dying and the stress from knowing unless a miracle happened my blood test would come back HIV positive, was causing me to have heart palpitations.
"Kendra did you know you can contract HIV from anal, oral, and from vaginal sex, no matter the length of contact if your partner is infected?"
"John, I know you want to educate me but what's the point? I'm dead now. I ruined my life and I'm just waiting for the results so I can let Eric know what he's done to me" I said, as I put my face in my hands hoping to evaporate.
"Please don't think like that. I can help you with so many things. There are women, mothers…"

When I heard the word mother, the virus became even deadlier. I couldn't imagine telling my girls I was infected. How would they respond-would they touch me or love me anymore? Did they even know what it meant to be HIV positive? No matter what they did or felt towards me I wouldn't blame them because I brought this upon myself."
"John, I'm scared…I really don't know how to tell Charles."
"You have to tell him the truth. This virus can't survive when people are educated and aware of what's going on inside of their bodies. That's why testing is so important. If you want I'll be right here when you tell him. Do you have any safety concerns?"
"I have all types of concern John...I've never had to tell anyone I had HIV!" I said as the words felt so powerful that they knocked the wind out of me.
"I understand, I'm sorry if it came out that way. I meant no harm."

The woman who rarely cried had turned into a crybaby and I couldn't cut the faucet off. How could I utter the words, I cheated, and how could I look into his eyes knowing my infidelity would lead to our demise and my death.

When Charles re-entered the room, John told us he wanted to give us some time to talk, and then he excused himself. Charles kept putting his hand on my shoulders saying it would be okay. I couldn't understand how he felt comfortable with touching me. I felt so dirty. I tried to pull away but he sternly said "No", and began to hug me as if all the love he had in his heart could cure me. But he still didn't know the truth and I had to tell him. "Charles…I cheated", was all I could get out and his hand reached for my face and I braced myself for the hit. However, instead of knocking my head off my shoulders he pulled my face closer to his and said "I know and we can get through this." My tears were so heavy that I felt like I was bathing him with them. I couldn't stop sobbing and neither could he. He was trying his best to console me and I was trying to take my mind off of finding a sharp object to cut my jugular.

Before I had walked into this office I was feeling great. I was ready for Charles to remove the condom and I wanted to move on with our marriage. I wanted to put my past behind me but now my past was every moment of my future. Just as quickly as I had decided that we were going forward it was clear that our future was over. Nothing in the world could have prepared me for this day. All my thoughts were about loss, failure and regrets. I wanted a can of fix-a-life but they only sold fix-a-flat. And talking it out didn't seem logical because this didn't seem like something Dr.

Calloway could repair. All this because I wanted to play pay-backs with Eric's infected ass!

Fingers Crossed
Chapter 10

Nothing really mattered to me anymore; not my job, the bills, bathing, eating or sleeping. I stayed in my room for two consecutive days, only getting out of the bed to use the bathroom. I was hoping and praying for a miracle that would change my test results. Every time my phone rang I'd look to see if it was John, but he still hadn't called yet. Just maybe the rapid-swab test wasn't accurate and maybe I would have a true reading with the blood test. Then maybe I was lying in my bed like a corpse getting accustomed to the grave I would soon be permanently in.

The depression and anxiety ruling my body was kicking my butt. The girls were frustrated because they wanted to know why I wouldn't talk to them or come out my room, so Charles made up an excuse. He told them I was very sick with the flu and it was contagious. I felt more like I was contagious and although John and I discussed transmission of the virus not being passed through kissing, touching, or hugging, I didn't want to put my girls at risk. Charles was the only person who entered the room and I made sure I kept the door locked at all times. I wasn't in a position to explain to Kala or Kyra what it meant for their mother to have HIV. I had the medical definition and read article after article on my laptop as I lay in my bed. However, for me I didn't know what being HIV positive would mean. My entire lifestyle would change just as my mind was changing.

I didn't know what to do or who to turn to and these were my constant thoughts. I wanted to call my mom but the embarrassment kept me from dialing her number. I felt solitary confinement was my only option for now. Currently, three people-John, Charles and I-knew of my disaster. And in a few more days, if the test results had not changed a fourth would be added to the need-to-know pile. Eric would have to be informed of what he had done to me. I wasn't sure where things would go from there, or what the outcome would be, but I knew he would be delivered the overwhelming news.

Charles questioned me about Eric but what did he want me to say? I had slept with someone and put my life in jeopardy. There were no excuses and I didn't feel like doing anymore apologizing…after all it was I alone that was now suffering the dire consequences. Every other moment I imagined Charles packing up and leaving, or never coming home from work because he couldn't handle this. I tried to think of him and his inner wounds, and the burden he faced staying with me, but my mind kept telling me I was jumping ahead of myself. That I should wait for the phone call because if you think positive, positive things happen. But every time I thought of the word positive it made me feel like the test would be positive and I should stop kidding myself.

Nothing was stable, not me or my situation and I knew it. Charles didn't feel uncomfortable sleeping next to me but I didn't feel too good about it. I felt petrified when he cuddled up next to me and I felt he pitied me, but I didn't want his pity because that wasn't the type of woman I am. If he had any real feelings for me he should have put a pillow over my face and ended it.

Day three of my waiting came and the uncertainties had now turned to reality. The last time I was in the office with John I gave him my permission before I left to reveal the results over the phone, as long as I gave him the code-word 'Liver' when he called. I didn't want to suffer the embarrassment and agony of going back in to the center, and being in my own home was a better environment for the good or bad news. The call from John officially confirmed my worst nightmare. I didn't know if I was shocked because I had so much doubt. If both of Charles' tests were negative, how much faith could I have in getting a negative blood test? Those tests were 99.9 % accurate, whether salvia or blood was used, so why had I hoped for a different outcome.

John was as comforting as he could possibly be and for what it's worth I appreciated it…but it didn't do me any good. He wanted me to come in for immediate aftercare but my mind wasn't ready for treatment. I still was trying to attach three letters to my name. When I hung up I knew I wasn't ready for my reality. This was a matter that I didn't know how to handle and I didn't want to handle it. Why did it have to be me? I mean I wasn't a whore; I didn't shoot up any damn needles. I had an affair and I know that's bad but I know women and men who have slept with so many people they could build a social network, but they didn't have HIV. I wanted John to call me back, apologizing because he had made a horrible mistake. I'd be a bit upset but I'd forgive him because I would be clean and free of the traumatic effects of HIV. I wanted Charles to walk into our bedroom and look me in the eyes and say, "Baby your life isn't over, it's just beginning." I wanted a fairytale but I wasn't Sleeping Beauty; I was fully awake and infected with a deadly virus.

As I lay in my man-made bed of death I thought about my girls. How was I going to look into their soft-brown eyes and tell them why I didn't want them to drink or eat after me? Oh, and that they could not kiss or touch me. I started to smell myself but I didn't have the energy to bathe. I wanted to try and clean myself up so I could have a talk with my girls when they came home from school. I thought about my life-insurance and luckily I had it already because I doubt if they'd give two-hundred-fifty thousand dollars to an HIV infected woman. Who would raise my children? Would Charles continue to care for them as he had done? I didn't know what to think. He had loved them and treated them like his own, but if he didn't want to I'd have to confess my sins to my mom. That meant full disclosure and I was still struggling with deciding who needed to know.

Since I knew Charles hadn't given it to me, it was time for me to reach out to Eric. I had delayed calling him until I got the call from John but now I was sure I was infected and so was he. The last time I talked to him I told him it was over. He was upset and said I had strung him along, but I didn't see it that way. I never promised him anything and this was my first affair. Look what it brought me- nothing but deadly results. I had always been so careful and very selective and now I had to warn Eric. I didn't know if I wanted to physically harm him or if I could forgive him. I seriously doubted that he knew he was spreading this virus but I had to let him know. My mind and heart wouldn't stand for letting another person suffer the same fate I was dealing with. If telling him stopped the spread to another woman, I was ready to let him know.

The first time I called him I blocked my number and hung up as soon as I heard his voice. But it was only his answering machine, so I called back and got the message system again. I thought about telling him over the answering machine, hey at least I would have done my part but I knew that was inappropriate. I just had to get him to answer. I figured he was ignoring the calls because the number was blocked, so I unblocked my number and called three more times. Nothing changed though; I got his answering machine three more times. I called one final time and left a message for him to call me back as soon as possible because it was important.

Two hours had passed and I still hadn't heard anything from Eric. I hope he didn't hear the message and get scared thinking I was pregnant or anything like that. The girls and Charles would be home in less than three hours and I still hadn't found the strength to get up and get myself cleaned. I walked into the bathroom and the mirror was the first thing that noticed me. My hair was all over the place and my eyes had bags deeper than a six-foot grave dugout. It was unbearable seeing my face in the mirror and I quickly turned away from it.

As I removed my clothes and stepped in the shower I felt as if the virus was staining the tub. Each time the water hit my body, I felt like I had been sucker punched. I fell to my knees and cried out to God. Why had this happened to me? I was never promiscuous. Yes I had made a mistake, but damn! Why of all things did this had to be my payback? Why couldn't I get a batch of crabs, syphilis or even herpes for that matter? All of them seemed like a blessing at this point, but instead I was cursed. I never hurt anyone; I never stole, or really had ill will toward the world. I loved my girls, I was a good mother and I went to work every day. "Why God, Why Me?" I cried endlessly as the water continued to hit my body.

I did my best to grab the soap and wash my body. I didn't get up off the tub floor; instead I sat and cleaned myself. It was much easier this way because my legs were too weak for me to stand. I never once touched my vagina because I was disgusted with it. I didn't even dare dry it off with the towel; it was just too repulsive to touch. Charles used to tell me how pretty it was but now I'm sure he thought it was nothing more than a monstrous death trap. My breath stank and I forced myself back to the mirror and began to brush my teeth. Never before had I brushed my teeth without looking into the mirror. It was a ritual I did to ensure every tooth had been removed of plaque. But when I looked in the mirror I swore I saw the grim reaper behind me and I began freaking out. I was losing it but I had to keep it together. I looked under the sink and found the bleach and without gloves I began sterilizing the entire bathroom. I didn't dilute it. I took the cleaning rags and began pouring bleach on them and then wiping everything down. I wiped the walls and when the paint began to peel off; I added a little water to the rags. By the time I got to the toilet the fumes had taken a toll on me and I fell down. I inched my way to the window and opened it fully to get some breathable air in the room and into my lungs. Initially I felt the room was cleaned but I wasn't satisfied, so I threw away all of the old toothbrushes and wash cloths Charles and I had used, along with the soap, shower caps, and robes. Then I left a note on the bathroom door for Charles that said 'Showers only, do not take baths!!!' Luckily I had my own private bathroom in my bedroom because I couldn't have shared a bathroom with Kyra and Kala.

When I was done my phone rang and I sat up on the bed to see who it was. It was Eric and I didn't want

to answer but I had to tell him. The first time I let it go to my voicemail. Maybe he'd leave a message. He didn't and I wanted to call right back but I didn't know how to deliver my unsettling message. I'd just have to tell him the truth but who would he tell, I thought. I wasn't about to disclose this information to him if he couldn't keep his mouth shut. I had to protect my children and myself. I picked up the phone and I called him back but when a woman answered the phone, I immediately hung up. What the hell was going on? Was this dude spreading this virus to every chick in the world? The phone rang again and I picked up.
"Hello."
"Yes, you just called here."
"Yes, I called for Eric. Is he available?"
"Not right now, but can I take a message."
"No…Who is this?"
"His mother" she said swiftly.
"I'm very sorry; I just didn't expect a woman to answer his phone. Is he okay?"
"Not in my world he ain't…that boy done got himself locked up. He said someone was gonna get in touch with me about some bail money, are you Raina?"
"No, that's not me...Do you know when he's getting out?"
"Nope. And if he don't get this money I damn sure ain't puttin notin up. He'll have to sit. I love my kids but I'm on disability. I'm barely making it my damn self."
"I understand…okay thank you so much. If he calls please tell him to call Kendra."
"Okay."
"Thanks, goodbye."
"Bye now."

Eric was in jail. What in the world had happened? I had to find out. His mom was causally holding a conversation with me and she gave out some details, but I needed a full report. Toni came to mind and I quickly gave her a call but she didn't pick up. This just wasn't my day, my week, or my damn year. I had a migraine headache the size of Africa so I took two Tylenol PM's, along with a shot of absolute. For now I needed to rest until I could figure something out.

Peek-A-Boo: I'll Come Find You

Chapter 11

Charles was enraged to the point where he wanted to hit me. The more he tried to get me to see his point of view; his frustrations peaked because he couldn't convince me to jump on the same page with him. He wanted to know why I had to go to Toni's instead of dealing with my situation. But little did he know I was dealing with my situation the best way I knew how. I had to go. I was on a mission to find Eric and let him know what he was carrying in his blood stream. Maybe I'd feel better after I told him, maybe I wouldn't, but either way he needed to know. I didn't want him spreading this shit to anyone else. However, I wasn't ready to tell Charles why I was going to Toni's. He already knew I was having an affair with someone from Raleigh but I doubt if he knew I was going down to confront Eric. Whenever he brought up the topic of the affair I always became teary eyed and the sympathy he felt for me, allowed him to put a lid on his suspicions and walk away. And whatever he was feeling now had to be pushed aside because I had to make this trip.

At times I felt like I needed Charles more than anyone in the world. He was the only one who knew what was really going on with me, and he did everything in his power to comfort and provide for me. It had been two and a half weeks since I last went to work and I had no inclination as to when I'd return. Truth be told I was not mentally or physically ready to return, and fortunately for me I wasn't in any financial turmoil thanks to my savings as well as the money Charles brought home. One evening my boss made a trip out to the house, and thankfully Charles was there to iron out the situation. I could hear her downstairs telling him how concerned she was about me and how valuable I was as an employee, but they needed to know when I'd be back to work. Charles let her know I'd be in touch as soon as I felt better to give her a definite answer, but I had no clue when that would be. John had written me a note, which allowed me to be out on short-term disability. However, he wanted me to get in touch with my primary doctor so I'd have something a bit more official if I was going to be out more than three weeks. I still hadn't managed to get up the courage to tell my mother or my daughters, and the thought of having my family practitioner staring at me and treating me as if I had a deadly, contagious, strain of Ebola-confirmed I wasn't ready to make that move. For now, John's letter sufficed but I knew the time would come when I'd have to fess up to my family doctor or go back to work.

After a few hours of yelling back and forth, Charles threw up his hands and said, "If this is the way you want to live your life, then go ahead...You're the one making this harder than it has to be!" I wasn't listening to what he was saying because deep down inside, I knew he was only staying around out of pity. How could he love me? I felt he had love for me and the girls, but he wasn't in-love with me like he was when I didn't have the virus. I'd never be able to give him the child he so greatly desired and we'd never be able to make love again, so what did we really have? We weren't sleeping in the same bed because I didn't want that and he started using the girls' bathroom because he was tired of me bleaching down the entire bathroom after I used it. It felt more like we were roommates rather than husband and wife. His words meant nothing to me and all I wanted was for him to take good care of the girls until I came back home.

As I made the five hour drive to Raleigh I wondered if I'd get to see Eric. I knew I'd be back in his town but I didn't have confirmation that I'd actually link up with him, or even make a phone connection. When Toni had finally returned my calls, she told me I was always invited to her home, when I expressed to her my need to come back down for a visit. When she asked, "What's wrong?" I knew I was filled with depression and I felt so heavy, but I tried to lighten up. We had so many problems in the past and I didn't know if Toni could or would be able to keep my secret. This wasn't a baby shower or a surprise party, this was an immediate -excuse me, let me run away from her infectious ass- type of thing. I didn't want to make the wrong decision because I was not in my right state of mind. I decided once I got down there I'd find Eric and do my best to keep this to myself. For the moment Toni would have to accept my response that I just really needed to get away.

Toni was still at work when I got to her apartment. So I used the spare key she gave me and let myself in. I was so tired from worrying, from driving, and physically exhausted that when I sat on the couch I felt the inevitable happening. For two hours straight I slept, without any interruptions. When my cell phone rung, waking me from my sleep, I saw it was Charles and I texted that I was alright. He responded okay. I was in shock at how deep of a coma like sleep I was in. I couldn't sleep in my own home because I never felt comfortable, and I was always worried. But here I had finally found some solace. Either that or my body had taken over and given itself what it needed. Still I didn't have much of an appetite. So instead of making myself something to eat, I sat and watched TV. Besides that would have been a trip, because Toni didn't have any plastic ware and I didn't know if I'd have to throw away the dishes I used.

Law & Order: SVU was on and it was really a tear jerker. It disgusted me to see how people could even consider physically hurting children in any form, but it also made me think about how I was hurting my girls. I desperately wanted to explain to them what mommy was going through and what could happen, but I hadn't accepted my own reality. As a matter of fact, not only had I not accepted it, I wasn't sure of what my reality was. I didn't know how long it would be before I'd be coughing, skinny, skin dark and discolored, and or dead. As the idea of my funeral entered my mind, Toni came bursting in the door.

"Hey Girly, what's up?" she said, smiling and looking bright and cheerful as usual.

"Stuff, but how was your day?" I said, in a depressed and restless tone.

"Same day, different shit" we both laughed because Toni had mangled the saying.

"You know you look a mess…What's going on?"

"I need to get in touch with Eric." I responded, looking away to take attention off my now teary eyes.

"Oh, shit, you're pregnant!" she said, as she walked over to the couch and rubbed my belly.

"No, I wish it was that easy."

"Then what, I know you aint starting that stuff…"

"What stuff?"

"That distant stuff, you holding out now?" she asked, as she stared into my eyes.

"No Toni, I just want to get in touch with him because….he gave me something."
"Something, he had to give you something serious for you to drive all the way down here. What's going on Kendra?"
"Let's just say I can't get rid of this…"
"You got herpes! I'm gonna fuck him up…his dirty ass!!!."
"No…" I paused and every tear I was holding back jumped out my eyes.
"He gave you the HIV?" she asked, hoping to hear a no.
"Yes."

I had told her. It wanted to come out and as soon as it did, I immediately feared she would tell someone. I wanted to rewind the clock and maybe I should have said he gave me herpes, and that would have been better than HIV. She sat next to me on the couch and put her arms around me. At first she didn't speak and I didn't look at her. I held my head down and allowed the trickle of tears to turn into a steady flowing river. Did I make a wise decision? I prayed this would never happen again. I didn't want to run around vulnerable, telling my secret every time someone asked me a few prying questions. She hadn't even drilled me and Toni could be relentless, but either way she knew now. And what she wanted to do with this information was just another burden I had to carry.
"Kendra I'm so sorry…I want you to know I love you and you don't have to worry…you will be okay." she said, trying to sound convincing.
"Toni, that's easy for you to say, you're not dying…"
"Stop that! You ain't neither... Did your doctor tell you that?"
"No, but I'm going to die eventually..."

"So am I! But you don't see me asking death to come pay me a visit any sooner than it has to. You know what you have to do…you have to find out how to live with this. Don't treat it as a death sentence but as a different way you have to live your life."

"Girl, I don't even know if I want to live…"

"Well whatever you don't know, know this… Kyra and Kyla want you here forever. You have to take care of yourselves for them."

"I shouldn't have told you."

"Why the hell not?"

"Because what if you get upset with me and tell somebody."

"Now come on now…this ain't something you go around telling people, okay. I know I can be a bitch at times but I've done a lot of growing, haven't I?

"Yeah, I guess..."

"Shit ain't no you guess, keep it real."

"You're right but Toni just promise me that you won't," I begged.

"No I won't! Ever! Is Charles okay?"

"Thankfully, he's fine. It's crazy we started using condoms after he gave me that shit and that's what probably saved his life."

"Kendra, you sure?"

"Yes girl, he's been tested three times."

"Listen you're not in this alone. You can't hold something like this inside. I could hear the pain in your voice when you called and I can sure see it in your eyes. That's a lonely road to travel and a heavy burden to bear… I got your back Kendra, we're sisters."

"Thank you." I said, as the tears began again but the weight lifted a bit.

Time flew as we lay on the couch and I explained to her my dilemma. Eric was in jail and I needed to know his last name and what prison he was in so I could contact him. Sadly, Toni didn't know his last name nor did she know how to get in contact with her old friend Masood, because his number was disconnected. She had no knowledge where either one of these dudes lived and I felt like such a fool. I had lain down with a man who I couldn't identify but he had left his DNA (Dirty-Nasty-Ass) killer sperms all up inside of me. I tried calling Eric's phone back, with hopes his mother would give me some more information on him, but his damn phone was disconnected too. I felt hopeless and defeated. My entire reason for coming down here was to identify the culprit and stop him from hurting other women. But I had failed and now I didn't know which way to go.

The next best thing for me to do was drink. I was scared to use Toni's glasses, so I asked her to take me to the Dollar General to pick up some paper goods. When we walked in the store and she saw what I brought, she got upset. "Girl you ain't contagious. What the hell is wrong with you" she boldly whispered in my ear. I didn't know what to say and I put my items down and walked back to the car. I wasn't trying to give her anything. She had been kind enough to listen to my pain, to lift my spirits up a bit, and I only wanted to protect her.

Once we got back in the house, Toni started making me a peach margarita, sugar-rim of course. She asked me to come off the couch and into the kitchen so we could talk.

"The first thing I want you to know is that you can't give anybody HIV by using their dishes. Didn't they tell you that?"

"I know but I have to be careful."
"There's careful and then there's overdoing it and you're more on that line."
"Listen, I'm just scared…"
"I know you're scared but you can't live like that. You're gonna need some help, someone to tell you what's going on?"
"I'm okay…"
"Really…I've seen enough Lifetime movies to know you're being paranoid and causing more damage than you know. Stress is a killer and you don't need any more than you have. And don't even worry about Eric. God knows how long that boy will be in jail. Besides he's going to know because they have to test him for that before they let him out into general population. Trust me I know everything because Rasool schooled me on all the in-and outs of prison life. He'll know soon enough…if he don't know already."
"You're right…"
"Just worry about Charles and my nieces, and you!"
"I know."
"Are you scared he's gonna leave you?"
"No, actually I want him to leave me…I don't deserve him."
"Don't do that, this could've happened to anybody."
"Well why didn't it, why did it have to choose me…"
"Kendra, we're going to get through this. Drink up" she said, as she handed me my drink.

In the morning, when Toni left for work, I got on the computer and goggled as much information about HIV as I could. There were so many sites, with so much information that I kept thinking I'd find some new information about a cure if I kept myself up to date. I found multiple chat-rooms that I could log on to anonymously, which I liked because I felt safe living in secret. I wanted to connect with people who knew and could feel first-hand what I was going through, but I didn't want them knowing my name or any other identifiable information. And even though it was good to have Toni on my team she had no clue what it felt like to walk in my shoes. I wanted to know what I was in for and to find someone who was willing to give me some advice on telling my children. So I searched a number of sites and read through some of the post by other people infected with HIV:

I'm in a really bad situation, I was in a really bad abusive relationship and we were both addicts. I was single for almost 2 years after I got away from him, then I met the man of my dreams! We aren't perfect but he's wonderful and I really love him! The problem is I tested + for hiv and haven't told him yet, I don't know how to!? I live with him and his family, I don't have any family or really anyone that can help me! So I'm in a pretty bad predicament. If I tell him and he breaks up with me I have nowhere to go and I haven't wanted to be sexual with him bc of the situation. It's putting so much stress on me and our relationship! I hate myself so much, I can't even get out of bed most days, I know my ex infected me and I really think he knew and didn't care. I don't want to hurt my bf like that in any way, that would make me just as bad! But I love him so much n he's my life! I don't even have anyone to talk to about any of this! Please help!!!

Scaredgirl24

I WAS TOLD THAT I HAD HIV IN 1999 I WAS 16 AM 24. NOW WITH TWO KIDS THAT ARE HIV

NEGATIVE-NOW WITH THAT SAID I NEED TO KNOW WHY IS IT THAT WHEN PPL KNOW THAT YOU HAVE HIV THEY LOOK AT YOU LIKE YOUR GOING TO GIVE IT TO THEM. I AM SEEING THIS GUY THAT I BEEN SEEING FOR THE LAST 2 IN A HALF YEARS WHEN IS A GOOD TIME TO TELL HIM ABOUT ME.

UNSUREANDAFRAID

Gay infected and still the shit.
GAYBOY93

Hoping my baby doesn't have HIV. She is only three weeks old and I didn't take any HIV medication while I was pregnant. I been using drugs and just realized I have to get myself clean. Hope it's not too late.

Biggestfuckup10

Just found out my brother has HIV...what can I do? I hate him now he's dirty and I don't want him to touch me. I want my mom to kick his infected ass out of the house. I don't even eat at home and I'm ready to go live with my friends just to get away from him. I should throw his medication away so he can die sooner...He is an embarrassment to my family!!!

Lizy55

I want to end this life they call mine. I've done all I can to do better, therapy, taken my medication and I'm still depressed. I love my children but I'm not loving me anymore. I want to do it myself but I'm such a punk. If anyone knows how I can do this quickly and painless please post to me...I'm always on here anyway-I got no life.

16candles

Been living with HIV for many years and still kicking. Thanks to my new meds and a great diet, oh and don't let me forget my exercise bike...I feel healthier than I have ever felt. HIV isn't my end-stay positive y'all!!!

Loveroflifeinspiteof

After reading a few of those posts I realized there are so many people living with HIV and we all have different fears and obstacles to accomplish. On the Centers for Disease Control website they stated that there was an estimated 1.1 million people in the US living with this virus. The number is probably higher than that because everyone hasn't been tested and there are confidential in-home test, which don't have to be reported to any medical centers. Then I thought about the number of people affected by someone being infected with HIV. The family, the spouses, and the friends all suffer. This was much bigger than I had wrapped my brain around.

My search for more websites continued and I found a site dedicated to helping parents tell their children about their HIV infections, as well as ways to protect them. One site that I found helpful asked the parents questions which could help you in deciding if you should or should not tell your children. Such as, how important is confidentiality to you, and will you children be able to keep your secret? The answers to those two questions were my biggest concerns. I didn't want the girls running their mouths off to our family or their teachers or friends. That would not only hurt me but could also put a stigma on them and I didn't want that. They didn't do anything and I wanted them to have a normal childhood.

One more piece of advice the site gave, suggested I know all I could about the virus before beginning my conversation with my children. Being newly infected and trying to come to terms with the virus I knew some things about HIV, but I'd be lying if I said I didn't have more questions of my own. I decided that I needed to get back home to talk with John and see how I could live my life with HIV and then I'd worry about telling the girls later.

After leaving Toni a note on the fridge, I packed my things and made my way to the car. She'd been more than what I'd expected and gave me some inspiration to keep moving forward. Now I was going back home to find this way of living she recommended. And although I was leaving Raleigh without connecting with Eric, he wasn't a dead issue but he'd have to be found at a later time.

One Day At A Time
Chapter 12

My first day back at work was noticeably strained. I couldn't focus on my reports and whenever a customer complained and wanted manger assistance, I gave them a verbal lashing without hearing their side. Most customers are cool people who just want their liquor and they're quickly in and out of the door. On the flipside there are those who have nothing better to do than put all their problems and misery on others. Not today! I just wasn't in the mood for it. So when Lexy called me out of my office to speak with a customer whose complaint was, she didn't like the attitude of my cashier, I was already on edge.

"Mam, what seems to be the problem?" I asked.

"Well your cashier", she stopped and rolled her eyes, "has a nasty disposition and I don't appreciate being mistreated."

"How exactly where you mistreated so I can correct this situation?"

"Well there's no exactly, it was just her mannerisms. She probably shouldn't be working with the public!"

"And you probably shouldn't be using big words you can't spell or define. If you don't have a valid reason, such as her saying something to you inappropriately or throwing your items in a bag, then you're wasting your time with me. My boss' name is Lisa and I'll give you her number if you want it."

I stood there waiting for her response as she eyed me up and down. I wasn't feeling her stares so I said, "What?" Then she grabbed up her bag and rushed out the store. Lexy had a surprised look on her face because this wasn't my normal reaction to my customers, even those who were outright unruly and wrong. As I begin to walk back into my office she asked if I was okay. Of course I told her I was because there was no way she nor any other of my co-workers would know what was really going on with me. A fool would think that she asked out of concern but I knew better. Too often jobs are filled with nosey bums who only want to learn all they can about you to use those things against you; and our job was no different.

I was still trying to concentrate but no matter how I tried I couldn't focus on my damn report. Charles was scared that I was going to have a nervous breakdown, so he kept calling me every half-hour to check on me. There was no way I was going to have a nervous breakdown at work, because I did care about my image and the role I played at my job was about being a leader. By closing, it had become clear that I was in need of counseling if I was going to return to work on a permanent basis. I had given in and contacted John and made an appointment to see him on Saturday.

Early Saturday morning I got myself ready for my appointment and this time I came in with pen and paper because I needed to get all the facts I could about my illness. I still hadn't told the girls and I never forgot the advice I got from the website.

"Morning Kendra, how you holding up?" John asked.

"I've been better but I'm okay."

"Good. Well I understand you have some questions?"

"Yes I do. I keep thinking I need to tell my girls about what I'm going through. Well not what I'm going through but I want to let them know what I have."

"Okay."

"I want to make sure that I know as much as I need to so they won't be scared."
"Sure, I understand that. I have plenty of handouts about talking to children in addition to the facts about HIV. They clear up any myths that are out there and explain transmission as well as how not to contract the virus. Are you sure you want to tell your girls…how old are they again?"
"They are eleven and eight…and I just want them to know so they can understand why I've been so protective of them lately."
"Well, I want you to consider their age because they are rather young and I don't know if at that age they will fully be able to understand. Also I've talked to you about confidentiality a lot. Children don't always keep things to themselves that we like, so consider all these things before making your final decision.
"I appreciate that because God knows how I'd feel if they would let that get out to their teachers. I'd never be able to show my face at another PTA meeting."
"I understand your fears but there are parents who are open about their status and they've had no problems. Also Kendra I want you to consider going to group counseling-and have you started taking meds yet?"
"No."
"No what?"
"I haven't started any meds yet…"
"Oh no…why not? Did your doctor say you shouldn't?"
"No, I'm too embarrassed to tell my doctor. I don't want that written down in my folder. What if that gets back to my insurance company and they drop me or cancel my life insurance?"
"Kendra you are overreacting. You don't have to worry about getting medical care, the state has to care for you,

and you need to manage your HIV. Without the proper medicine and treatment your viral load will rise."

"What is a viral load?" I asked, feeling stupid because I thought I had read and remembered that term from one of the many sites I goggled.

"It's the amount of active HIV in your body. The count is very important because it lets us know if your immune system is at a greater risk for opportunistic infections."

"Oh…"

"Yes, we want to keep your viral load as low as possible. Your viral load can be measured with an Ultrasensitive HIV Viral Load test that would range from 50 copies to 75,000 copies or they could use a Quantitative HIV Viral Load and the results vary from less than 400 copies to greater than 750,000 copies."

"Well what was my count?"

"I don't have a count on you. Your doctor has to order that blood test" he said, as he quickly browsed through the thin manila folder before continuing, "And you want to be seen so they can gage your levels quickly. With medication and a reduction of your stress, I'm sure you can stay healthy and fight this. But you have to start getting treatment."

"I will."

"Are you going to see your doctor or do you want me to refer you to facility."

"Refer me…please."

"Sure, but I want you to know that you don't have to feel embarrassed about this. I know it's hard for you to hear but you are not diseased or dirty. You have HIV but you are still a beautiful, decent woman who deserves the same respect as any woman who doesn't have it."

"Thanks, John."
"Anytime. I have a list of doctors you can go through; I'll give that to you. All they do is treat people infected with HIV and AIDS. Also I want you to visit one of the group sessions at The Circle of Care. That's a really good group and you won't feel alone or out of place."
"Really…"
"Yes really. They all have HIV or AIDS and no one judges each other. I've sat in on quite a few meetings when I first was diagnosed."

John had confessed. The virus was closer than what I thought. I had felt a bond with John. I trusted him and I never looked at him funny for obviously being gay, because I wasn't a homophobe. Now he had let me know we had a deeper connection than our love for shoes. It was a relief to see someone living and looking healthy but now I had more questions than when I first came in the door.
"John I'm sorry, I never knew…I mean you never told me."
"Don't be sorry. And discretion for me is about choice. I wanted you to see that HIV can happen to anyone. You'd be surprised who has it. HIV doesn't have an age group or color preference, or gender for that matter. It strikes when it strikes but the medical world has come a long way. The new meds are great. They truly will help you maintain a healthy lifestyle and for many they may never see their HIV progress to AIDS."
"Yes…I can only hope I'm that lucky."
"Well you can only do that by getting on meds. I take four pills a day, two in the am, and two in the evening. I don't have many side effects and it's so important to take the medication as prescribed. There's no skipping pills or changing times. You don't want the virus to build up resistance to your meds."

"I didn't know all that…"
"Well I want you to get in to see a doctor as soon as possible. The earlier the treatment the better the outcome. I'm not sure what meds will work for you because I'm not a medical doctor but trust me they will come up with a treatment program that works for you. Now promise me you're going to get on some meds."
"I promise."
"Okay, and don't forget the group."
"I won't."

I got up from my chair and was ready to walk out the room, and then John stopped me and said, "Discretion. It was my choice to tell you, now let's keep that between us." I looked up and said, "I would never break the bond we're building. Your ability to trust me has made it easier for me to keep moving forward. I can't thank you enough but I'll say it again; thank you John and I appreciate you. "

On the ride home I felt reassured knowing John was finding his way through this scary obstacle in his life. He hadn't let it stop him and he was helping others get over the hugest hump in many of our lives. I respected him for trusting me with his private and personal information and I vowed to never share it with a soul. John had helped me make the difficult decision of getting on medication and I promised to give group therapy a try. My fear of being seen by someone I knew was still a major factor but I had to give my body a chance to fight this virus physically and mentally. I knew seeing and talking to other people who had the virus would help me to live with the HIV virus.

When I got home Charles and the girls were sitting in the living room watching something on TV. I quickly said hello and then I ran upstairs because I hadn't used the bathroom when I should have at the clinic. I didn't like using outdoor toilets but now I was paying the price because I was like five seconds from peeing on myself. When I entered my room I realized my bedroom door was left open. As I sat on the toilet I looked at my medicine cabinet that had been left open. When I was finished using the bathroom I look into the cabinet and saw one of my razors has been removed. I started to panic. Why in the hell was my door open? Had Charles used my razor? He knew better…Oh shit was it the girls!!!

"Charles come here!" I screamed, as he began running up the stairs.

"What's the matter?"

"My razor, who used it…where is it?"

"I didn't use it."

"What do you mean you didn't use it…why was the door open!"

"I must have left it open and maybe one of the girls came in…."

"Nooooooooooooooooo!!!!!!" I shouted.

"Kyra and Kala come here!" he called, as they came running up the steps.

I collapsed on the floor because this wasn't happening. My girls meant everything to me and there was no way I could live with myself if one of them had used my razor. I know they were young but maybe they had tried to shave their legs. I didn't know. I couldn't think straight. I was in a panic.

"Mom what's the matter" Kyra said, as she tried to wipe my tears.

"No don't touch me" I screamed, scaring her and causing her to start crying.

"What did I do mom" see cried, and Kala looked at me confused but trying her best to comfort her baby sister.

"Nothing baby, you didn't do anything. I just have to talk to you girls."
"Not now Kendra, this isn't the right time." Charles interrupted.
"Charles this is the time. Girls I have to ask you two a question."
"Okay," they said.
"Who touched my razor?"
They looked at each other but didn't respond.
"Its okay girls, I'm not mad…I just want to know who used it."
"I did mom." Kala said, as she hung her head.
"What did you use it for!" I shouted.
"Calm down Kendra! Just calm down!" Charles demanded.
It dawned on me that I was scaring them, but I was scared too.
"I'm so sorry but please tell me what you used it for." I begged.

Kala walked to her room and returned with her baby doll. The doll had both sides of her hair shaved off.
"Mom I only used it to give her a Mohawk", she said, as she begin crying as she passed me the razor. She had been begging me to let her get a Mohawk but since I said no she gave her hairstyle to her doll baby.
"Let me see baby, let me see." I said, as I examined her hands making sure she hadn't cut herself.
"Listen girls I want you to know why mommy has been so stressed and why I've been in my room lately" their eyes widened, like they had been waiting to find out.
"I have been very sick and I don't want you two to catch what I have."
"What is it you have mom" Kyra asked.

"Kendra no, please not now." Charles pleaded.
"It's okay Charles, trust me. Girls what I have is like a cancer but I can get help for it. It's something my doctors are working on so I can be better, but I need you to do me two favors…okay?"
"Okay mom," Kyra said, as Kala repeated.
"You can't use my things because you can catch it. It's harder for doctors to treat my disease in children, so please girls don't use my razor-even though Kala you used it to do an awesome haircut-I just don't want to take any chances because you could have cut yourself and caught it. And I don't think you girls would use my toothbrush or washcloths but to be on the safe side, don't use that stuff either."
"Mom ill, that's just gross" Kala said.
"Yes it is gross so don't do it."
"We won't" Kyra said, and then she asked what was the other favor.
"I want you to keep this between us. No one has to know that I'm not feeling well because it's none of their business. I'll be okay and I don't want them to worry…okay?"
"We won't" they agreed and then I asked them to for a hug.

That was a huge step for me because they hadn't had physical contact with me in a month. I missed them, the way they smelled, the feel of their skin, and now I finally was able to stop freaking out and hug them tightly.

I had dodged a serious bullet and I wasn't about to let something like that happen again. I had taken my razors and my toothbrush and found a lock-box to put them in. Only I had the key so I didn't have to worry about them getting into the box. I had already stopped anyone from using my bathroom and we didn't share dishes. Everything in our house was plastic-ware, except for the cooking utensils. It might have seemed extreme and I was well aware of the transmission of my virus, but I had to do all I could for the safety of the girls.

Charles was very relieved that I hadn't completely fessed up to the girls. But I knew after my conversation with John that they weren't ready to hear the whole truth. What I had told them was good enough and if the time was ever right, I'd tell them if I felt they needed to know. For now I was thankful to God to have two children uninfected with HIV and I was willing to do whatever it took to make sure they stayed that way.

Expect the Unexpected
Chapter 13

Before I got a chance to make it to my appointment I had come down with a very bad cold. Doing my online research I knew I had nothing to fear because you often get flu or cold like symptoms during the initial infection, but my immune system would be able to fight off the illness. So I pushed on and continued to go to work daily and kept trying to stay positive as I waited to see the doctor.

Tuesday evening came and my first appointment was at PHILADELPHIA FIGHT, on 12th and Locust Streets. This building was a comprehensive treatment center, which provides primary care, consumer education, advocacy and research on potential treatments and vaccines. Everything a person needed who was living with the virus was there. They had physicians, case managers, psychologist, as well as a full running lavatory. I was being seen on the 5th floor at The Jonathan Lax Center to get my meds, and I was comfortable with going to this center. This was a safe house for people infected with HIV & AIDS. It was all about treatment as well as providing resources for us, and many of the staff members were living with the virus as well.

I won't say that I had totally gotten over my fear of being spotted. So on my way in I made sure I had on a hoddie and a baseball cap, to hide from anyone I might have come in contact with from the outside world. I even made my appointment at 6:00P.M. because I figured many people would be trying to get home, instead of coming into town. The center closed at seven, so that gave me enough time to get in, get out, and go unnoticed.

Upon entering the building everyone was very polite. The security guard welcomed me and was very helpful in pointing me in the direction of the elevator. When I stepped off the elevator and made my way to the registration desk, it was very quiet. I was the only one in the waiting room and the receptionist was not at her desk when I first entered. I waited just a few minutes before I said, "Excuse me" then I saw her rush over to register me. She joked about trying to sneak in a smoke break, and then she asked if this was my first visit. Upon agreeing she handed me a clip board with two forms to complete. Then she asked for my insurance card before telling me, "You can have a seat it will only be a few minutes." Being there I felt like I was normal. I mean in the world I now lived in I was an outsider but going into an environment where most people there shared a common factor, made me feel at home-in a sense.

Less than five minutes had passed and I was being called to the back. I hadn't even finished filling out the forms, but the woman who registered me told me she'd pick them up from me before I left. I was ushered into a small examination room, where the nurse took my blood pressure, temperature-without gloves-before asking me to get undressed (everything but bra and panties) and to put on the pink robe she passed me. It was so cold in that room. I know they wanted to keep the germs down but you can't kill the virus with a chill, so a little heat wouldn't have hurt anyone.

By the time the doctor entered the room, which wasn't much later; I had completed my medical forms and was ready to be examined. She pulled up her

spinning chair as I sat upright on the examination table and she smiled slightly before shaking my hand.
"Hi Kendra, I'm Dr. Barnebey. How are you doing today?"
"I'm doing okay, thank you."
"Great. Let me wash my hands and I'll get started. First I'll listen to your heart and lungs, and then I'll do a look-over."
"Okay." I said, as she began her exam.
"What medicines are you taking?"
"That's why I'm here, I'm not on any."
"Oh, we can help you with that. Not every doctor places their patients on antiviral medication in the beginning but I do. I prefer to be diligent against the virus and with the new medicines that are out; they are making a world of difference. Did you get a CD4 cell count yet?"
"Huh… is that my viral load count?"
"No, that's different. Two blood tests are often used to monitor people infected with HIV. One test counts the number of CD4 cells, and lets us know your immune system is still functionally properly. The normal range is between 500 and 1600 cells per cubic millimeter of blood and your count should fall within that range. The other test determines your viral load and that directly measures the amount of virus in the blood. I know it's a lot so are you still with me?"
"Yes. I'm still here."
"Great. Well this first test is the baseline test. It will let me know where you're at with your levels and let me know if I need to change your initial treatment. Then you'll be tested in about four weeks after treatment so I can see its effective, and every three to six months after that you'll be tested to monitor your progress. I'm

going to have the nurse do your blood work. Any questions so far?"

"Yes, what happens if my levels falls under 500?"

"Well if that happens we need to do some very aggressive treatment to help prevent opportunistic infections, such as pneumonia. We have to be very careful because let's say someone has a CD4 count fewer than 200, their HIV has progressed to AIDS. And we do not want that."

"Will my count be that low?"

"Kendra, I doubt that very seriously. This is a new infection and from what I can see, you are not in that range. But we will do a count because we have to monitor these things in our patients. Also I don't want you to become obsessed with numbers. It's my job to help you stay in the best health and you have to help me with that."

"I am going to do all I can; I want to be well for me and my girls."

"Great, and if I place you on medication it's a lifelong commitment. You have to take it the same time daily and exactly as prescribed. I know it's a lot but we do all we can to assist you."

"I understand."

"Okay, all looks well" she said, just as she finished looking over my legs and arms for any abnormalities of abrasions. Go ahead and get dressed and I'll send the nurse."

"Okay."

"By the way have you seen anyone in our mental health department?"

"No, I don't think I need that right now. Besides I've been seeing a counselor and soon I plan to go to group sessions."

"That's great, but if you feel you need to, just know we have some of the best people here to help you with the transition. I know it's a lot for someone to find out they have the virus and then to go on living with it can be harder than the diagnosis. It can take your body and mind through a lot of changes, so please let us know if you ever, ever need our help. After all that's what we're here for."

"Thank you" I said, as Dr. Barnebey removed her gloves and trashed them, before heading out the door.

On the ride home I kept looking at the prescription and the pamphlets I collected from the waiting room. I rode past a 24 hour Walgreens and a Rite-Aid but I didn't pull over to get the prescription filled. There was no way to hide from the Pharmacist and their staff, because I'm sure if you worked in that field you'd know what HIV meds where. It was only seven fifteen and I wondered if I had come back to the Walgreens around midnight, would it be empty. I'd be able to dodge most of the people, any traffic but that still left handing the prescription to the Pharmacist. I was pissed that I couldn't have my meds filled at my office visit; after all they were a full comprehensive center. But Dr. Barnebey explained they only had medication on site for individuals who didn't have medical insurance, or for medical on-site emergencies. My last option was to ask Charles to drop them off and pick them up for me. I didn't see why he'd have a problem with it because his name wasn't on the prescription. However, since we shared the same last name he still could have felt some embarrassment because he was picking up HIV meds for his wife.

I quickly walked in to the house and greeted the girls who had been on the couch waiting for me to come home. I saw their partially eaten plastic dinner plates still on the table, but they had popsicles and chips in their hands. They ran up to me and hugged me, which was something I still had to get accustomed to. I was constantly reminding myself that I wasn't contagious and the virus couldn't be spread through kissing, hugging, sharing dishes, tears, air or water, or causal touching. As often as I read the literature it should have ceased my fears but with my girls I was always thinking of the what-ifs. If anyone was going to be protected from this virus, it was my girls.

Charles was upstairs resting. I was sure the shock of the virus still hadn't wore off and his commitment to help me out with the girls was taking its toll on his body and mind. He was still confused as to what he could and not do with me. Before he left out the house in the morning he'd kiss me on my hand or on my forehead because he was scared. It had now become a normal sleeping pattern for him to occupy the couch once the girls feel asleep. He made sure he was up before they got up so they wouldn't worry about our relationship or have conflicting thoughts. Our sleeping arrangement was what I needed to be comfortable because I could no longer share a bed with him. I wasn't happy in my marriage. I didn't know when my marriage would end but I knew the time would come real soon.

Wednesday morning before Charles left out for work, I asked him to drop of the prescription for me. For what should have been a routine response of a yes or no, had turned into a full mental breakdown. He started sobbing and asking me if I was dying. Of course I was dying I thought but not today, or for at least ten years I felt. Charles was unable to stop crying and I was getting nervous. He sat on the end of the bed and kept saying how sorry he was and how badly he wished this would all go away. I had wished the same thing, daily, minute by minute, second after second but I still had HIV. This wasn't the time for me to drop the ball and give into my sorrows. I had to find a way to live; especially if I wanted my limited years to be filled with purpose and bonding with my girls.

"Charles…Charles, please stop crying." I asked.

"Baby I'm just so sorry…you don't know. I'm sorry."

"This isn't anyone's fault and right now I need you to be strong for me. If anyone is sorry, it's me." I said, as tears begin to fill my eyes."

"Kendra, I'm sorry…"

"Charles, why do you keep saying that. I'm going to get through this. Is it the prescription because if you don't want to fill it I'll do it?"

"No." he said, as he let out a loud cry.

"Then let's just find a way to make it through each day. We can't play God, we just have to…"

"I have a son!"

The words were like silver bullets filled with holy water that pierced the heart of a vampire. I knew our marriage would end eventually but a baby. That was the one thing he desired and we would have had but thanks to the Depo shots and the Chlamydia, and now this damn virus we would never share that gift.

"A son?" I asked, as I felt my lungs fill with disbelief.

"Yes, I didn't know how to tell you but how can I deny my son?"

"So you've been seeing Dana behind my back! I told you I didn't want your fucking pity! You never had to stay! And when did this happen...How old Charles?"

"He's six months and I wanted to tell you before, but so much is going on."

"Yeah so much is going on…how long did you intend to hide this?"
"I don't know…I knew Dana would've called you if I didn't say something to you soon and I didn't want you to hear it from anyone but me."
"Thanks Charles, hearing it from you made me feel so much better. Better yet I
think I'll just go and throw you and her a damn baby shower. That's how good I feel about it!"
"Kendra, don't…"
"Don't what Charles? If you hadn't messed around on me in the first place I wouldn't be in this shit of mess right now. Don't what Charles!"
"For everything I've done I'm so sorry…I really have to let you know now I never meant to hurt you and for what it's worth I wasn't dealing with her, she just ended up pregnant. I begged her to get an abortion but she wouldn't."
"Right, she wouldn't…I wonder how convincing you were. I couldn't give you one and now I never can! So you really want me to believe you tried!"
"Yes, I want you to believe me. I really did try. And now she's keeping Charles away from me because I'm still here…and she knows."
"WHAT DOES SHE KNOW!!!"
"What was I supposed to do? I slept with her and I wanted her to be tested too. It's the right thing to do!"

"So she knows about me?" I asked, as the words scorched my mouth. It was one of those moments where you and a girlfriend stop being friends and you don't really give a damn; except for the fact that bitch knew all your personal business. Yeah one of the moments but to the hundredth power because the virus wasn't like she knew your secret about sleeping with one too many guys, having an affair or having a drug

problem. This was the ultimate secret and Charles should have never leaked it! I mean why couldn't he have found another way to get her to take the test.
"Kendra, don't worry she's not going to say anything."
"How the hell can you say that?! Does she have a permanent muzzle on her mouth, because if she couldn't keep quiet about having your dick all up inside of her why would this be any different!"
"It's a lot different…"
"How?"
"I'm going to be gone by the end of the week. It's the only way she'll let me see my son, and she'll keep quiet I promise."

He grabbed the prescription from the dresser as he walked downstairs and told the girls to come on. I had not anticipated this. A baby and now he was going to move in with Dana and their child. Did I have the right to be upset-legally he was still my husband-and was he serious? He walked out the door and I knew it would only be two more days before he was gone. What would I tell Kyra and Kala, what would my family think? Was this just the beginning of the end of my life? Would I be able to live without my current support system? Did my boss actually think I was going to make it in today? Well I answered that question quickly as I removed my shoes and sat on my bed; flooding my mattress with tears.

Pills, Pills, Pills-Oh and Side Effects
Chapter 14

As promised, he left on the weekend and Kyra and Kala both knew the truth. He had called himself filling them in on Friday when he picked them up from school. They were crying their little brown eyes out, begging him to stay as he packed and begin putting his bags in the car. I walked them into their bedrooms and told them to stay put until I had called them out. I was done crying for him. He was hurting the people I loved the most and I was going to be strong for them.

Although it was eating me up on the inside that he was doing this, I couldn't stop him. He had gained something more precious than our marriage, his little Prince Charles Jr. A few times while he was in our room packing, I let out my frustration by punching him in his back and kicking his legs, but my punches didn't faze him. He was a man with his mind made up and this was the end of us.

On the dresser he left a detailed letter of things he'd be helping me out with until we fully resolved our relationship. I laughed when I realized our marriage was now being referred to as something as minute as a relationship. Good ole Mr. Charles was going to make sure he deposited fifteen hundred a month into my account, and he'd continue to pay my car insurance, as well as keeping the girls and me on his health insurance. In that same letter he also informed me I would be removed as the beneficiary from his life insurance, because he wanted his son to get the bulk of his estate. He was listing Dana as the fiduciary, until his son turned eighteen. Also he wanted to pick up the girls every other weekend but I wasn't having that. I had no idea where she lived at and I seriously doubted he'd give up that pertinent information.

Before he left I asked where he'd be staying and he kept silent, so I knew my girls would not be doing any weekend visits. Besides, why would he want them there anyway? We weren't some happy blended family; my family was being torn apart. My husband abruptly left me without listening to my opinion or considering my feelings. Towards the end of the letter he kept saying my illness had nothing to do with him leaving. Who was he trying to convince? He must have thought the virus affected my brain, but I wasn't a fool. I guess in reality he was a man, with needs, and I wasn't satisfying him. With her, his sexual appetite would be fulfilled and now he'd have a family of his own. There was no longer any need for me…there was just no longer a need for me.

My prescription, which he had gotten filled, was left on the dresser as well. I guess I should have been grateful to him but I was still in shock. Since the day he told me he was leaving I hadn't been back to work and the calls from my boss were pouring in. I wanted to tell her I was heartbroken and infected but I knew better. So I told her I wasn't sure what had come over me but I was too sick to come in. I could sense her frustrations in the tone in which she spoke, but she kept her cool and demanded I bring a letter back in from my doctor. A letter was going to be produced for sure, because I wasn't going back into work anytime soon. I had enough leave on the books to be out sick for at least six paid weeks, and anything after that I didn't care. This time I had to be out from work until I really got things in order. My health, mentally and physically, and I had to cope with this new loss. When I first got my diagnosis I had lost my mind, then I felt my womanhood disappear and now my husband bailed out. But if I was going to be successful in life I had to learn to accept the things I couldn't change and keep on moving.

I begin to read the medical information for my pills ATRIPLA. I heard many horror stories where people had to take almost fourteen pills a day to fight their HIV infection, but I was lucky enough only to have to take one pill a day. My viral-load and CD4 count was stable, which allowed me to be prescribed these tablets. The medication combined three HIV medications in just one pill and it was proven to lower viral-loads to undetectable levels. As I read the common side-effects of dizziness, headache, trouble sleeping, drowsiness, trouble concentrating, and/or unusual dreams, I realized I had them without taking any medication. The other common side-effects included, vomiting, gas, diarrhea, tiredness, and upset stomach. With any new medicine I expect the body has to make adjustments to tolerate the medication, but nothing listed on this label was too scary. The medical pamphlet went on for about two pages, talking about what medications to avoid while on ATRIPLA-which were other HIV meds- and when to stop taking the medication-if you were or become pregnant and if breastfeeding. I couldn't imagine anyone trying to get pregnant if they were knowingly infected with HIV but to each its own; I guess. For me the risk far outweighed the reward.

I made my way downstairs to get a bottle of Poland Spring water. The medication had to be taken daily, at the same time, and on an empty stomach. The pamphlet also stated taking the medication at bedtime may make some of the side effects less bothersome. So I figured I take them at night because I'd be in the privacy of my own home and no one would see me popping HIV meds. Also I didn't want to deal with any unnecessary side-effects.

It was about seven-thirty when the bell rang and I rushed to the door, hoping to see that Charles had changed his mind and returned home. As I looked through the peep-hole my hopes were instantly crushed when I saw it was my parents. As I opened the door I quickly tucked my pills into my pants pocket, along with the medical information sheet. I wanted to know why they were here, but these were my parents and they were always welcomed. They quickly came in to escape the chill of the winter night and sat on the couch. Kyra and Kala came running downstairs, giving their grandparents a hug and asking them if they had come to pick them up. Since I hadn't heard anything about their plans I told the girls to go back in their rooms while I talked to them.

"Kendra, how are things?" my mom asked, as my dad sat there like she was designated to ask all the questions.

"Things are okay, what's up mom?" I asked, because I could feel they were acting strangely.

"We know you need our help now, we love you and we are here for you."

"Mom, what are you talking about?" I asked, sitting in confusion.

"Charles told us everything. He didn't want to but he knew you needed someone" she said, as she tried to put her hand on my shoulder, but I pushed her away.

"Charles told you what!" I shouted.

"Kendra, calm down the girls are upstairs", my dad said.
"Dad what did he tell you?" I repeated, as he hesitated to respond.
"We know you have HIV and that he's gone", my mom whispered.
"Why the hell would he tell y'all that!" I shouted, as I leap up from the couch.
"It doesn't matter, no one is judging you. We're here to help" my mom said.
"It's like he's broadcasting my personal business on the six 'o' clock news!!!" I said, as I begin to fill myself becoming overwhelmed.
"No Kendra, he didn't have anyone else to turn to and he cares about you. Besides he knows we won't tell anyone" my dad said, as he stood up and wrapped his arms around me.
"Well dad, I pray you guys don't tell anyone. I mean that…nobody. Too many people know already!"
"Never baby, we'd never do that to you. We don't want this to get out any more than you. We're just here to help you out. Let mom and me take the girls for a while. They're going through a lot too", my dad said.
"They must really be feeling the pain now that Charles is gone", my mom said.
"No, I can't burden y'all with them. They are my responsibility" I said.
"We are a family Kendra, don't fool yourself girl. It's been Charles who's been helping you with them lately, and I know you've been down and out of work lately," my mom said, as she began to dive into parent mode. I hated when she called me girl or girly, but at this moment I knew she was right. I had always been this independent superwoman, who never needed the help of my family-even though it was always there. But I

needed to loosen up and give in to their request and let them help me.
"Okay…but only until I get myself together. I love them and don't want them to feel like I've abandoned them too."
"Never. Besides Kala called me and asked us if she could come over. She probably just wants to spend some time with us."
"She did?" I asked, as I sat back down hoping I was doing what was best for them.
"Yes, and they'll be fine. We can take them to school and everything until you get on your feet", my dad said.

I went upstairs and told the girls to get them some things together because they would be staying with their grandparents for a while. They both seemed excited and not the least bit concerned about leaving me. I had turned into a drag, nothing more than an energy zapper. I knew they needed to get away from me until I had found some piece of myself. Before Charles left I was on the right path. I had a bag full of positivity and I was going to find my way. Even with him gone, I couldn't give up completely. I had to try and convince myself I had something to live for.

I helped the girls gather up their clothes and shoes in their suitcases, and then I carried the bags downstairs. My parents were there for me, I kept telling myself that. I didn't want to think about how Charles had violated my trust, more than once, and I needed to lie down and fall asleep as quickly as possible. Once my dad took their luggage to the car, the girls hugged and kissed me and ran to get into my dad's black Ford Explorer. My mom looked into my eyes and told me, she'd take care of the girls and I didn't have to worry about anything, before hugging me and walking out the door.

I knew my girls were in great hands. Both of my parents were retired and had nothing but time on their hands, and money to spend on their granddaughters. My father had made his living by owning and operating a string of Laundromats, until he got in his sixties. Then he sold them to a man in Ohio for a price that has him sitting pretty comfortable. My mother was the soul food catering queen. She worked so hard and had made a reputable name for her company. She has been invited to prepare food for some of the wealthiest citizens in Philadelphia. My mom worked so hard that she can no longer wear the five inch heels that she loves. Her feet are bad from all those years on her feet, so now she has to settle for a well-padded flat.

My parents lived in a three bedroom near 29th and Popular, and I knew my girls would enjoy staying at their home. They loved our city and had some great connections with our affluent neighbors, so I knew they could expose the girls to events and people that I could respect. More importantly my mom and dad had morals and were loving people.

When I closed the door I felt alone, abandoned, and betrayed by Charles. I reached in my pocket and pulled out my pills, then walked to the kitchen to get my bottle of water. However, once I had taken it I realized I was in need of something more, therefore I reached into the cabinet and pulled out a bottle of absolute. I took four straight shots, before finishing off the bottle of water and making my way to my bed.

As the week progressed I had been on my meds with no physical side-effects. Dr. Barnebey had faxed over medical documentation to my boss, requesting six weeks off due to a temporary disability. My boss had called me several times trying to suggest alternative work schedules. I let her know she was wasting her time because I wasn't coming back until my six weeks had ended. After two days of her calling me and trying to convince me to come in to work, she reluctantly accepted my medical leave request.

I was unable to sleep nights and I was having panic attacks, along with severe suicidal thoughts. I confessed this to Dr. Barnebey, when she called me on Saturday for a routine follow-up call. She called in a few meds to the ACME pharmacy on City-Line Avenue to help me deal with my new set of issues. I was now taking WELLBUTRIN for my severe depression and EFFEXOR for the panic attacks. With both I was to take one tablet, two times a day-with or without food. She also prescribed Trazodone to help me fall asleep and stay asleep; and that was one pill a day, two hours before my bedtime. In less than two weeks I had gone from one pill a day to six pills daily; which added up to forty-two pills a week. Soon I felt the effects.

I had diarrhea and intense itching, as if I had scabies under my skin. I woke up one morning and my gums were so sensitive I couldn't brush my teeth because the medium-soft bristles felt like a hard grill brush, and the slightest touch caused my gums to bleed. When I took anxiety and depressions medications without eating I vomited. Both meds said they could be taken with or without food but if I didn't put at least a few pretzels or crackers on my stomach, they'd bring up everything I had eaten. When I did have a regular bowel movement, the color had changed drastically. It looked pale… pearl white and that scared the shit out of me. I was back and forth on the phone with Dr. Barnebey. She asked if I had taken any other drugs than the ones prescribed and I told her no. She suggested I continue the medications as prescribed until my body had gotten use to them. However, if I hadn't gotten better in a week or so, she wanted me to come back in to the office to see if she needed to make any changes to my meds.

Actually there was one thing I had added to my prescription regime but I didn't use that much of it to cause a problem. Absolute was so soothing at night and it made my stomach settle and eased my mind. I enjoyed taking two or four shots of it a night. Even though some of the labels of my meds said the slightest use of alcohol could result in negative side-effects. I realized the real side-effects came when Charles walked out on me. The hell with the label's warning! Had my life never been imprisoned by this incurable illness, my side-effects wouldn't exist.

The Circle of Trust
Chapter 15

My job had medically terminated me and this was just fine by me. After my six week leave request ended I didn't return to work. Instead Dr. Barnebey requested I stay out for another six weeks. Upper management made the decision that I was definitely replaceable and let me go. The initial letter they sent demanded I come back or I'd be let go, and when I didn't show up on the requested return date, my career with the State Liquor Board came to halt. My boss had signed the letter, along with the district manager and her superior. They had taken all the steps to terminate my employment, and when I got the certified letter I was officially dismissed.

I didn't care about getting fired. Although there were a few employees who were fun to work with, along with the crazy folks who made their way into our store on 2nd Street in Old-City, to purchase their booze. I would miss them but I'd get over it. My favorite customer was Mr. Spade. He was homeless but a day didn't go by where he didn't come in for a fifth of the cheapest vodka we had on the shelf; which was Nikolai. Spade never had a dollar bill on him and would take as much time as he needed to search his coat and pant pockets, socks, and his secret hiding department-which was a miniature wallet he kept tucked inside his pants-to count out his coins. He was pleasant and always made us laugh at his crazy stories, that he called 'Another Homeless Adventure'. Mr. Spade loved being homeless, well at least that's what he told me. He said he had no worries and life was much simpler without the stress of a mortgage, utilities, and financial burdens. Every day before he left the store I'd tell him to be safe, and if it was cold I'd say stay warm, and then he'd hold his bottle next to his chest and say, "I got my protector and some heat". Homeless or not he was a good man; funny and intelligent, funky too, but still a human being that I'd miss. Maybe with all my free time I'd ride pass the job and buy him a bottle or two, since I had plans to make occasional visits to the store when I was in the area.

Also I wanted to give Sonya a head's up. She was the youngest employee in our store, very sophisticated for eighteen, but she often had her face so embodied in a book that she slacked on the job. Once I found her sitting in the stock room, sitting on top of the boxes reading with her legs propped up, as if she was at home sitting on her favorite chair. Crazy part was it wasn't even her break. She was supposed to be gathering orders and taking inventory, but she couldn't put those books down long enough to get a full day's work completed. When I was there it didn't bother me. I actually supported her reading passion and would help her out when I had the time. But since I was no longer going to be employed there, I wanted to remind her she had a little one at home. She needed to focus on performing her duties because the next manager wouldn't be that nice. Yes I would miss that place but now I had ample time to work on me and my recovery.

Since I had so much free time and the girls were spending most of their week days with my parents, I contacted John and asked him to attend my first meeting with me at The Circle of Care. He had become an advocate for me and encouraged me to stay positive and to keep moving forward. They held daily support meetings at 6:30P.M., except on Weekends, so on a Thursday night he met me outside of the front of the building and escorted me inside. At first I was nervous as hell to get out of my car, and of course I looked to see if there were any familiar faces lining the sidewalks before I got out of the car. When I saw John I greeted him and began to walk into the building. But then my body felt heavy and I almost froze. He looked at me and said, "The longer you're outside the greater chance you have of being seen." It was funny but true at the same time, so we laughed and I quickly made my way in.

When we entered Suite 1000 I kept my head low and followed John as he spoke to everyone there, before he made his way over to Tracy. She was the lead counselor and the organized the meetings. If no one else in the room stood out, she sure did. Wearing a t-shirt that said '*HIV Positive & Proud of It*!' how could you not permanently brand that image to memory? She was a little thing, with a very motherly spirit and when she spoke you realized she was the real deal. She cared, she understood, she wanted to help you, she wanted you to live, she had hope and with her you were safe. She kept looking at me, as I tried to disappear behind John. And then she placed her right hand under my chin and lifted my head up. Then she said, "Nobody here is gonna hurt you…are you okay?" I smiled because I knew I was acting weird. I was tense and trying to get myself accustomed to entering those doors on a consistent basis. I didn't know what to expect, what I'd hear, how I would feel, but for the moment I was sure I could handle everything except sharing my story.

Tracy looked at the clock and realized that it was six thirty. She quickly called for everyone's attention because she was ready to start the meeting. Everyone in the room began arranging their chairs in a pattern to form a circle before having a seat. John sat next to me and I was sitting next to Tracy. But then she stood up and walked in the middle of The Circle of Trust and began the meeting. She introduced herself, then asked everyone in the room to introduce themselves clockwise, until everyone had gone. I was sitting right next to her, so I was second and I barely spoke loud enough for me to hear myself. So she asked me to repeat my name and then John followed. With the introductions done she stood up and said, "There are more than five new faces in this bunch of twenty-two, and I'd just like to say welcome. Know that here you are not going to be judged, and this is a place strictly for healing and learning. So if anyone isn't ready to share, I'd like to start off tonight's meeting." Everyone was eager to hear her story, along with the regular group attendees, and with our approval she began.

"Again, my name is Tracy and I've been holding these meetings for the past six years. I've been living and fighting this virus for over ten years and I've had some victories as well as some defeats along my way. Today is the anniversary of my husband's death" she paused, like his face had just appeared in her mind. Then a few tears fell from her eyes and she used her hand to wipe them away. "Teddy and I used drugs and we both shared needles, and did things that I'd never do with a sober mind. If I didn't lose my daughter, I probably wouldn't have found out we had HIV. I shot up my entire pregnancy and at first I didn't know I was pregnant, but when I did find out I didn't stop and I didn't get prenatal care either. She came three months early and was so tiny you could barely hear her cry. They had all types of tubes hooked up to her and she barely weighed two pounds. Just looking at what I did to her made me quit, but it was too late. She was a fighter. Not only was she fighting HIV, but she was addicted to heroin and going through severe withdrawal. For ten days my little girl gave it her best but I had given her my worst, and that was more than she could bear. When she passed my husband was in the streets getting high, and I was somewhat high because the doctors had to give me methadone until they could safely wean me off of heroin.

Seeing her tiny body lay there…I was done. I felt guilty because I had killed my daughter, not the HIV. She didn't stand a chance and with one loss came another. When I left the hospital my husband wasn't able to quit using and join our fight against HIV. Heroin was his god and he shot up until God called him home. I don't ask why anymore because the why don't matter. I've spent the last ten years of my life fighting and watching my body suffer from poor health. I had a hysterectomy last year and I went toe to toe with meningitis. I've met some really good people in my line of work; and I have attended some funerals and memorial services of those I've worked with also. But I'm not discouraged because I've gone to a few weddings and baby showers too. I've been lucky enough to hold babies whose parents have HIV but those beautiful babies don't. HIV may have entered my body and tried to steal the life out of me…but guess what-I ain't done yet!"

The Circle applauded her fighter spirit as John hugged her and she sat back down in her seat. I now understood why boxes of tissues were placed on a small table in the middle of the circle of trust, and I was so overwhelmed with her ability to share such a personal story that my tears almost suffocated me. One by one everyone in The Circle shared their stories. Some people stood up, other sat and all their stories were different. Some made you laugh, others made you think, and then there were the ones like Tracy's that touched a place in your heart that made you breakdown. But all the crying wasn't about pain and misery, it was actually healing. As I sat there, knowing tonight wasn't my night to spill it, I still felt lighter. Just being in a room with people from all walks of life and all races and backgrounds, who all shared HIV as our mutual connection was powerful and therapeutic.

When it was all said and done, I didn't share that night and no one made me feel that I was obligated to. This room was where you could feel protected and there was no pressure. Afterwards John mingled with everyone and I went up to Tracy to give her a hug. It was like Mr. Spade had always told me, "Just when you think you're shit is bad, there are always others who are worse off."

I was thankful that I attended my initial meeting and to John for being my escort, because the experience kept me attending. As scared as I was of being recognized downtown, where you never know who you could run in to, I fought my ego to get into those meetings. I met new people who were just like me and all they wanted to do was help others, and themselves. We learned about new medications and Tracy kept us abreast of the latest HIV and AIDS breakthroughs. She also made sure we signed petitions to fight for more money from congress for HIV/AIDS research. She believed a cure was coming and if not in her lifetime, she'd be able to rest easy in her grave as long as one came.

As much as I enjoyed the meetings and trusted the sanctity of The Circle of Trust, it took me just over twenty visits before I had the guts to open up. I sat because my knees were weak. As I began to speak it felt like I was sitting in a courtroom, on a witness stand giving my sworn testimony. My group members were like the jurors, watching my every movement and hanging onto my every word.

When I looked into Tracy's supportive eyes I found my courage. They reminded me of where I was and who I was surrounded by. We were a family and I had nothing to fear. No one was going to go running around shouting I had HIV, because we all did. We all wanted to be accepted and loved. This was my moment. The time when I let my guard down and let them know what Kendra was feeling and how I was coping with my diagnosis. The nerves had vanished and now I wanted them to hear me and to see me for who I was. I wasn't some diseased, disgusting woman. I was a mother, an abandoned wife, a daughter, and a woman who wouldn't rest until I found out who had brought HIV into my life.

The Grapevine
Chapter 16

The girls stayed with me at the house while on their Christmas break, and since Toni was on vacation until two days after the New-year, she had come up too to keep me company. I was enjoying their companionship and I realized how much I had missed all of them. We went shopping and out to eat, and at night Toni and I enjoyed margaritas-with sugar rims-yeah you know it. Everything had been progressing well and I wasn't having any health issues. The group meetings kept me focused and there were times when I was alone and missed Charles.

I wondered about him and wanted to know how his baby was but I didn't have the guts to call him. It was crazy because we were legally married and usually married people feel as though, as bad as it sounds, there is some type of ownership over their lucky prizes. But for me I was in limbo. He had kept his word and placed his monthly stipend of fifteen hundred dollars in my account, which was the one thing he was capable of being faithful to. For the month of December he added an additional two thousand dollars for the girls Christmas gifts. He also sent them Christmas cards but they never saw them because I ripped them up and threw them in the trash. There were times when they both asked about him but what was I to say. I really felt it was better to silently lay him to rest in all of our lives. Eventually I knew he'd have to get in contact with me, especially if he was ever going to marry Dana. He'd have to divorce me first and I would not contest it. But for now I was okay with the way things were.

On Christmas day my family always gathered at my Aunt Maggie's house to celebrate, exchange gifts and eat dinner. Although I wasn't family orientated, I enjoyed making the short trip to Cheltenham Township to relax in the comfort of her five bedroom, two and a half bath rancher-which was situated on a crescent road- surrounded by acres of land and other lavish homes. It was a time when I could see the new editions to our family, listen to the latest gossip and laugh at the family misfits: Aunt Poochie, who always drank too many Budweiser's and with her weak bladder it was inevitable that she'd have an accident, and Uncle George the klepto who couldn't help but steal something even if it was family photos, both provided many hours of amusement. The gathering was a combination of Thanksgiving and Christmas in one. My Aunt Maggie was a great cook and she threw down a southern style feast, and took no short-cuts. Everything was big and plentiful, down to the desserts.

Originally, I wasn't going to go because I didn't want to be the latest gossip. However, after talking to Toni-who always knew the latest family business-she assured me my mother and father had actually kept their mouths shut about me. Not that I thought they wouldn't, but letting the cat out the bag wasn't going to be as easy as speaking in group. My family's house was nothing like The Circle of Trust. It was more like a soap opera, where more than a few people thought their shit smelled like roses, and no one hesitated to take a stab at you if you were careless enough to leave your personal business unguarded. But since Toni reassured me, we got the girls ready and made our way from the Main Line to Aunt Maggie's.

When we pulled into the driveway it was filled with cars and the street was lined with my family members' vehicles as well. The girls were so excited they couldn't wait to jump out of their seatbelts and run into the house. Once I found a parking spot we walked down the driveway and entered through the back of the house. The bottom level of the house was just as luxurious as the top. My Aunt Maggie had just remodeled her home to include an outdoor pool, small pond and a full entertainment room in the basement-along with a nice sized bar.

As we entered I begin to see the cheerful smiles of my family, and as suspected Aunt Poochie was already slouched on the couch with four empty beer-cans sitting on the table in front of her. All of the adults in my family had some type of cup, bottle, or can in their hand. No one in my family drank soda except for the children. My family was full of alcoholics. It was no wonder where my taste buds came from.

Toni took all of our coats and hung them up as we made our way upstairs to see who came through this year. Once upstairs I saw my mom and Aunt Kelly sitting in the living room, thick as thieves, as usual. They both had a glass and from the color I assumed they were sipping on Southern Comfort. My mom was a bit shocked when she saw me because she thought I wasn't coming. I forget to call her and let her know instead of Toni bringing the girls, I would be coming too. She got up and asked to talk to me for a minute but I didn't feel like talking. My mom had recently become a worry-bot and she always wanted to know how I was doing. I kept telling her I was fine and she was babying me too much. If I walked in the door by myself, with no help, she had nothing to worry about. But she insisted I walk with her to the bathroom. So Toni excused herself and walked to the bar to make us some margaritas. As we walked to the bathroom Charles came walking up with a little boy in his arms; which had to be he son.

This was my family's house right? There were over thirty adults in this house and almost twenty something children running around having a good time…why in the hell was he here? As he continued to approach me, he stopped and said hello and asked if I had a moment for us to talk. Talking…I hadn't talked to my husband in months. Now he was standing in the hallway, holding his beloved son-who he had left not only me but my girls for-and now he wanted to talk. I kept walking to the bathroom with my mom as he continued down the hall to the living room. The nosey folks, also known as my family had seen our little interaction and begin the gossip mill. I didn't know what they knew about Charles and me, but I didn't care. He was an outsider and damn sure wasn't any part of my family.

When I entered the bathroom I made sure to keep my cool because it wouldn't surprise me if a few family members gathered by the bathroom door to listen in.

"Mom, are you serious?" I asked, as I tried to read her facial expression.

"It's not what you think." she replied.

"Okay mom, so what is it exactly? I mean let's clear this up."

"Girl, he just needed to see the girls and be around some good people. I know you're going to be upset but I invited him."

"You did?" I said, as my voice began to escalate.

"Yes, please keep it down. I had no idea you were coming. He just wanted to see the girls."

"Well he's probably seen them by now, so why can't he go back to Dana or go be with his family!"
"Kendra, he's not with Dana. She done messed around on that man something bad and he's staying in an apartment."
"Well how is that our business mom? He chose a whore so why in the hell did he expect her to be like me?"
"Kendra, your language."
"Mom, my language is mild compared to what I could be saying. You didn't have to invite him. He's been absent from our lives for how long now."

As I looked at my mom it appeared my last statement may have been true for me but she had been in constant contact with him since he was gone. To my surprise Charles had been a constant visitor at my mom's house and he still took the girls to school when he had the time. I was the only one abandoned by my husband and his motives still weren't clear to me. He wasn't my girls' father so why did he still want to be connected to them. I wanted to pull them into the bathroom and ask them why in the hell hadn't they told me, but I wasn't going to pull them into this.

After listening to my mom and her pathetic excuses for keeping this secret from me, I realized this wasn't why I had come to Aunt Maggie's. I wanted some ribs, a nice slice of the roast beef and to enjoy some margaritas. Most days I barely had an appetite and the Ensures were keeping me from losing weight, but tonight I was going to gorge and enjoy myself-regardless of my lying mother and Charles and his boy.

When I got back into the living room, Toni handed me my drink and whispered in my ear, "What the fuck is he doing here?" I was thankful that she was discreet because we all know how she can get. But with

Aunt Kelly in her presence she always found some self-control. I laughed it off and said, "Girl, we'll be up talking about this all night…okay", before I made way to the dining room to look at the spread. I made sure I said hello to Aunt Maggie, who was running back and forth from the kitchen to the dining room to keep the table stocked; and she was kind enough to make me a huge platter. Toni's greedy butt came running up behind me saying, "I want one too" and she looked at her and said, "You got hands don't you.

I told Toni to meet me downstairs because I wanted to get as far away from the girls as possible, and since the girls weren't ready to eat I wanted to mingle and relax. The fellas had the game on and they kept yelling at the TV screen and placing bets. This was another tradition and even though I wasn't into football I enjoyed watching while I was here. The couches and chairs downstairs were filled but nobody was sitting on the couch with Aunt Poochie, so I made my way towards her. She was still slouched over, slurring her words and trying to be a part of the football crowd. Two additional empty Bud cans had been added to the coffee table in front of her.

I sat my plate on the table because I had forgotten to get a fork. Luckily the small table downstairs had plastic ware, so I was saved the trip of going back upstairs and seeing his face. His son was so adorable and he clung to his father as I'm sure our baby would have. I did my best to quickly evaporate that thought from my head and chill-out and eat and drink. When I went to sit down on the couch, before I reached to pick up my plate, I felt moisture. Aunt Poochie had peed on the damn couch and now my pants had a wet-spot. I couldn't even get upset because that's why she was the only person sitting on the couch. Everyone knew about her. I went in the downstairs bathroom and washed my hands and used a wash cloth to wipe off my jeans. It made the small spot obvious but I didn't care because it would eventually dry.

I pulled up a tan folding chair and sat next to the coffee table and began eating my plate. Toni came down with her plate and almost sat on the couch with Aunt Poochie, but I warned her and she grabbed a folding chair. She looked at me and said, "She got you huh?" before we both laughed it off. She was ready to go in on Charles and his guest, saying how ugly his son was and how she thought he looked a little bit retarded. But I didn't want to talk about his son. He had nothing to do with his father or our relationship so instead of adding fuel to her fire I reminded her, "One day you'll have a child and you know when you talk about children yours come out messed up". As if that made her stop, but eventually she eased up when she saw I wouldn't bite the bait. She kept saying I was better than her, because if it had been her he'd be laid out all over this house, and my mom would be right along with him. But what would that solve? I still was a mother to two beautiful growing young ladies, and this was a night for us to get together in peace and happiness. I wasn't about to start no stuff, at least not tonight.

The drinks started to hit us and we had started dancing, and then we called the kids for a dance contest. My girls were pathetic. They had no moves and all the other kids were laughing at them. Drunkie, aka Aunt Poochie, made a comment that private school had sucked the black out my girls, but that had nothing to do with it. Their father danced like he had two left legs, and I knew they didn't get it from me because I could handle mine. Jazzy Lady had come on and all the old heads stepped on the floor to get their bop on. The back door had opened and everyone tuned to see who it was. It was Keyona and she was big as a house. I didn't know she was pregnant. Since Charles left and the girls were staying at my mom's mostly, I didn't need a babysitter so we didn't see each other much.

Keyona hadn't even taken off her coat and the whispers had started. Every time I looked someone was holding a private conversation about her, other family members, and probably about Charles and me as well. I didn't care though because the biggest secret was in the volt, and that wasn't going to come out no time soon.

After Keyona said her hello's and went through the house, she came back downstairs to sit with Toni and me. I didn't want to ask her any questions, besides was she okay and how school was coming along. But Toni and her mouth just can't be let outside of a muzzle. She was wearing the poor girl down and for a moment she started crying; saying how she was tired of everybody judging her. Really I didn't see the big deal. She wasn't a teenager, she was a young adult and she was still trying to finish school. I guess they felt she chose the wrong path and the holy-rollers were all caught up on her not being married. Either way I just wanted her to stay in school and make sure she was getting prenatal care. As she began to finish her dessert, she asked if I could give her a ride home when I was ready to leave. Something had come up with her boyfriend and he wasn't going to come and pick her up. Of course that wouldn't be a problem and we continued to talk and mingle with the family.

As the night drew to a close, everybody started to wrap up their take home plates and some took a few beers and wine coolers to go. But leave it to Uncle George to take it to another level. This nut had six damn plates, a six pack of beer, and he had the nerve to try and tuck a whole bottle of vodka in his sweatpants. My Aunt Poochie, drunk and all kindly called him out. "George you took enough food for a damn week but your ass ain't walking out here with that bottle!" He was on his way out the door, when my Aunt Maggie came over and extracted the vodka from his pants. Only Uncle George would pull this stunt.

Toni, Keyona and I helped clean up the downstairs. We tossed the trash in bags and folded up the chairs; and wiped off all the tables before we went upstairs to see what further help Aunt Maggie needed. The only people left in the house were Aunt Maggie, her husband Duke, Aunt Kelly, my mom and dad, Keyona, Charles, Toni, and the girls were asleep in the guest bedroom; along with Charles' son. The upstairs was pretty much clean, so I made my way to the kitchen to get some more food. It had been too long since I had good food like this, and even though Toni had already prepared our doggie bags, I wanted to have a small plate to eat before I left. I went in the bathroom and washed my hands and then came into the kitchen and started to make my plate. My Aunt Maggie screamed, "NO! Just wait a minute" and stared at me, before rushing into the kitchen to assist me. I was confused because what had I done wrong. Then it dawned on me. The volt had been opened and the gossip had gone through the vines, but I wasn't sure how far the news had traveled. She had offered to make my plate when her usual response was "make it yourself, you ain't no guest or you got hands don't you", and this year everything was plastic. My Aunt hated plastic and always enjoyed having girl talks, as the remaining helpers washed the dishes and helped her clean the house.

"So how many people have you ran your damn mouth to mom" I asked, as I sat the plate down and made my way out of the kitchen.

"Go on downstairs Keyona until we call for you" Aunt Kelly, told her.

"No, I'm going in the bedroom I'm tired. Just come get me when you're ready to leave, please" Keyona said, as she walked down the hallway towards the bedrooms.

"Mom, why in the hell would you do that. It's bad enough you invited Charles but spreading my business to the family, now you went too far" I yelled.

"Kendra, your mom had no other choice. She just wanted to be safe and Aunt Maggie is the only one that knows" my dad said.

"Oh really…Okay Aunt Kelly so what about you?" I asked, as she hung her head.

"Y'all some shit I swear! And if you was really trying to be careful you would have done your homework and found out you can't get it from sharing food" Toni said, protecting me.

"You know what, mom I'm done with you." I said.

"Don't do that Kendra," my dad chimed in.

"Oh don't worry I'm done with you too!"

Toni made her way to the bedroom and woke up the girls and they headed towards the car. I was really pissed and my mom and dad sat on the couch as if I had offended them. I mean if they were so worried and concerned that I was contagious why didn't they ask me to stay home. The remaining people in the house were looking at me with sympathy and I shouted, "I don't need your damn pity, I'm going to be okay!" Charles walked closer to me and I let him know he was the last person I was looking to for comfort. Before leaving I told my Aunt Maggie thank you and asked, "If you don't mind I'd appreciate if you kept this between us. I can't force you to keep quiet and if you think about spilling the beans just know that I have children to protect." She tried to assure me this was all a big misunderstanding and it was really about safety. I couldn't process what was said and I didn't want to. The two people, who were put on this earth to be my protectors, had sold me the hell out and there was no misunderstanding that.

On the ride home Keyona asked what the kitchen scene was all about and Toni let her know that it was none of her damn business; I told you she needs a muzzle at all times. I didn't feel like trying to make up excuses so I kept silent. Toni rambled on about what a messed up set of parents I had and about how she should have taken a bottle or two from Aunt Maggie's bar. When I dropped Keyona off, she said goodbye and said to Toni, "See you later little George". It was funny and had us laughing, especially since Toni had been running her mouth about Uncle George being such a thief.

Once in the house Toni helped me put the girl's in their bedrooms, before she went downstairs and watched some TV. I went in my room and lay on the bed. All my plans had suddenly changed because my first set of plans were to come home, eat some more of that good food and have a few more drinks, but now I didn't have an appetite. My mom and her mouth had opened up the gates for me to be the most talked about family member until the day I died. I was never going back to any more family engagements because I knew what would happen. In my mind I would be thinking only three people knew and then somehow I'd find out it was ten or possibly more. And that reaction Aunt Maggie showed me was too much. I wasn't contagious and I didn't need anyone around me to make me feel that I was. I was moving forward and now I had realized exactly how small my family and friends circle was.

I got undressed and jumped into the new pajamas that Toni bought me. They were really cozy and warm. I had been drinking and had a slight headache, so I was taking it down. Tonight Toni was on her own with her night owl mission. When I cut my lights off and lay my head on my pillow, my phone vibrated and I had a text message;

'I'm outside. Open the door.'

It was Charles…

New Year's Resolutions
Chapter 17

Toni wanted to go out to the clubs and party it up on New Year's Eve but I wasn't sure what I wanted to do. Keyona had agreed to take the girls to the Embassy Suites because they wanted to have a hotel party. She was on the outs with her unborn baby's father and needed something to do. Since she couldn't drink and was too tired to party, she was all too happy to make one hundred and fifty dollars to paint some toes and nails, do their make-up, and let the girls stay up all night drinking sparkling apple-cider until they tired themselves out. Now I had to decide whether I would bring my New Years in with Toni or my husband.

Thanksgiving night, after the dinner party, Charles had shown up at the house and wanted to talk. Surprisingly Toni encouraged me to go out and see what he wanted, but I felt her support was simply to get some hot gossip that night. He was begging me to understand his dilemma. He told me over and over how much he loved me and that he had no future with Dana, but how his son Prince was a big priority in his life. I could understand putting your children first and I felt his pain. I wanted him to be happy but I still was hurting. Trusting him was difficult if not impossible, because at the time I needed him most he walked out. I know he loved his son but why did he have to go back to Dana. In my heart I felt there could have been another way. He could have taken her to family court and fought for visitation rights, instead of allowing her demands to make him leave the woman he had vowed to love, cherish and respect until death do us part.

Dana was vindictive and he claimed that was the main reason he left me. Charles said he had tried to see his son on numerous occasions but was denied because he was in a marriage with me. He also said he was protecting me from her but he didn't want to elaborate on that comment; even though I tried to find out what he was implying. She was the last person I needed protection from and I would have fought with my husband to make sure he got visitation rights. I knew eventually if he didn't give into her demands she'd try to hit him with a child support order, but we weren't hurting for any money so Charles should have known I'd be there for him. I wanted to know what would happen if he came back home. Could we live as lovers or would we be like roommates again? I know I didn't want that because I wanted to be held and told I was beautiful and that my illness didn't define me. Also without question I knew Dana wouldn't let him see Prince if he moved back in. However, Charles insisted he was over her threats and claimed he was ready to be with me no matter what the circumstances. He swore on his life that he loved me and the girls, and that we were the perfect fit for him.

That night we talked for hours and ever since then we had been in daily contact, texting and talking; and we went out to dinner twice. Even though he pressed me to make a decision to let him back in the house, I wasn't ready. I didn't want him back home if that meant as soon as Dana got wind of us; he'd leave me again because he'd be cut off from seeing Prince. Presently it was enjoyable spending time with him because he knew what was going on with me, and I didn't have to explain to Charles my sudden moments of depression or my anxiety attacks. After a few internal conversations I realized I was struggling to come to grips with my diagnosis. Having Charles back in the house was what my mind and heart were saying I wanted, but I didn't feel as though my actions would represent my true feelings. I didn't want to have him home and then be the Wicked Bitch of the West. For now I had no choice but to take it slow because if I made another mistake in our unpredictable marriage, I just might lose Charles forever.

After giving it some thought I made the decision to go out with Toni. I told her that Charles wanted me to go with him and she told me to reconsider his request, because she and I could link up after the New Year. It was sweet that she wanted to see us work out our problems but tonight I wanted to stick with my New Year's resolution- to have a carefree, no worries start to my New Year. We both were dressed for the occasion, and even though it was a brisk, cold, New Year's Eve, we both had on skin tight mini-dresses. Toni wore hot red and I was in black, and we both had on fishnets and stiletto hills. And when I looked in the mirror I was thankful that even though I had lost a few pounds the Ensures had kept my curves where they needed to be.

We were going to have a ball no matter where we went because Toni had plenty of friends in the city and multiple parties to attend. We promised each other that our New Year's Eve was going to be a night where she and I could drink, dance, mingle and act as if all our problems or concerns didn't exist. Before we were about to head out the house, Toni asked me again if I was sure that I didn't want to spend New Year's with Charles. I didn't want to stare in the face of the man who had added to some of my depression, so I was sure. Tonight I only wanted to live life in a fairytale, filled with brown and light colored liquor and nonstop dancing. So around ten I let Charles know I was on my way out with Toni. He did sound disappointed and tried his best to convince me to change my mind but I wasn't motivated.

Toni and I made our way to our first stop, which was to one of her friend's party on the Main-Line. The woman's house was very elegant and the spread was abundant and delicious. I had never met her before or heard Toni speak of her, so I asked about her and was told she was just a friend that Toni had met in passing. She was a dirty blonde, Sharon Stone look alike, who wore a full length sequence burnt orange gown. For a moment I thought she was hosting or attending an award show, but it was her party and who was I to state the dress code. The woman was very happy to see Toni and she pulled her to the side and they begin talking. Immediately I felt out of place because I didn't know anyone there but I soon remembered my resolution and made my way to the bar. I stood in front of the beautiful marble bar countertop that she had built into her home, as I drank my margarita and waited on Toni. For about ten minutes they were exclusively engaged in conversation and I begin to talk, well I flirted with the bartender until they made their way over to me and made an introduction.

"Hello and how are you?" the dirty blonde asked.

"I'm fine and thank you for having us in your home, its beautiful" I said.

"This old thing…" she began to laugh.

"My name is Sue and it's a pleasure to meet a friend of Toni's."

"We're family, she's my cousin." Toni said.

"Well that's even better. Ladies tonight I want you to enjoy yourselves and if there's anything I can get you, just let me know."
"Thanks so much and I'm Kendra, it's very nice meeting you."
"Well I hope I can get to know you better Kendra", she said.

I smiled as Sue walked away and she began to entertain the multitude of guest that began arriving. I got a strange vibe from her and asked Toni if she was funny, and not because I thought she was hilarious but because she had a way of keeping her hands on Toni's waste as if she was her man. Toni denied it and jokingly called me a racist, which was far from the truth. I wouldn't say I had the best gay-radar but I was getting a few signals. Sometimes you can pick up on indirect invitations to the bedroom but maybe I was being paranoid. We took down two more drinks, then said our goodbye's to Sue before moving on to our next destination.

Our next stop was at a Latin bar in Old City, Cube Libre. Toni loved that bar and she got on my nerves when she pretended to be linked to their heritage through her bloodline. She was all black even with the few baby hairs in the front of her hairline, but she always swore she had some Latin ancestry. And maybe she did but with no proof I wasn't going to entertain her. Toni made a bigger fool of herself when she tried to speak Spanish with her African accent, but tonight she had me laughing and we were about to go be with her peoples.

Trying to park was a never ending nightmare, so we paid the twenty-five dollars to valet park. We immediately began to force our way through the crowd into the club, straight to the bar to gulp down mint flavored Mojitos. We both had taken down two without pause and then Toni wanted to dance. She was much taller than all the Spaniard men, who were the size of Umpa-Lumpas's on the dance floor. But that didn't stop her from moving her hips like a Latin ballroom dancer. She was shaking and moving her hips and I could see all the work she had been putting in on her stripper pole had paid off.

Before I knew it, an Umpa-Lumpa was grinding all up on the back of my legs trying to make his way to my ass. Since I wasn't that tall, if I had worn flats he would have been dead-on. I laughed at him but gave him credit for his effort. Then he asked me to dance but from all the grinding he was doing on the back of my legs I thought we already were. We made our way over to the crowded dance floor. The Latin flavor was different and definitely sexually infused. The more we danced the more turned on I became, remembering the passionate days Charles and I shared… I truly missed them. I hadn't had this kind of interaction in, I didn't even want to remember how long; and even though I knew it wasn't going anywhere further than the dance floor I was enjoying the vibrations that ran up my legs to my kitty-cat.

As the second song we danced to begin, I was now in the Latin grove and had begun doing the salsa as if I was now a professional. I was having a really good time and when I looked over at Toni, she had another drink in her hand and had now made her way over to a tall dark-haired man who initially was with a woman-or at least that is what I thought. My Umpa-Lumpa now had his hands all over me and thought I was going to dance with him all night. I wanted another drink and with the music so loud I damn near lost in my voice trying to scream to him that I was on my way to the bar, and with his heavy accent I couldn't make out what he was saying. So I made my way towards the crowded bar while he tagged along behind. It was so packed and at this point I didn't think anyone in the entire club had consumed less than five drinks. Everywhere I looked everyone was happy, kissing, hugging, laughing and just enjoying the evening.

When I finally got the barmaid's attention and ordered a mango mojito, I could feel my cell-phone vibrating in my pocketbook. I quickly reached for it but knew I couldn't answer it with all the noise. So I rushed to the bathroom so I could pick up before the caller hung-up. I didn't recognize the number because the area code was long distance and by the time I got into the bathroom I had missed the call. To my surprise the bathroom was empty and the noises didn't penetrate the bathroom walls. I decided to return the call but as I began to call the number back, the caller was calling back.

"Hello."

"Yo, what's going on Kendra?"

"Nothing much." I said, trying to catch the voice but I had no clue.

"So I guess you're a little surprised to hear from me."

"Yes, I guess you can say that." I said, still lost but playing along with him.

"My mom said you tried to get in touch with me but I had the hardest time trying to remember your number."

At first I was caught off guard but now I knew exactly who it was.

"Eric, are you out?"

"No" he laughed.

"Well where are you calling me from?"

"I'm still down but I got me a cell phone. My celly let me hold it. With tonight being New Year's Eve I wanted to reach out to a few people who had been on my mind."

"Oh, well I really want to talk to you and I had no clue you were locked up."

"Yeah shit does happen and I got myself caught up but I'm not doing life. Eventually I'll be out, you know."

"Yeah, well I've been carrying this around with me for some time and I did my best... Wait one minute." I went in both stalls and made sure I was alone, and then I squatted down in front of the entry door to block it because there was no lock on the door.

"You still there?" he asked.

"Yes. As I was saying...after I was with you I found out I was HIV positive."

It got quiet and now any drinks that I had consumed quickly made their way out of my pores because I was sweating profusely. At one point I thought he had hung up because there was dead silence, but when I looked at my cell phone screen we were still connected.

"Eric, I don't think you did this intentionally but I thought you needed to know."

"Kendra, I think you've made a mistake." he said.

"I made a mistake by being with you when I was married, and without protection, but that's the only mistake I've made. You were the only one."

"Naw, when I first came in here I got tested. Shit it's mandatory that everybody get tested so they can decide if you can go out in general population. They've got an AIDS ward here and I damn sure ain't on it. If I had it, it would have showed up on my test."

"So what are you saying exactly...that I'm making this shit up?"

"Naw, I'm not saying that at all. What I'm saying is I don't have it."
"Eric, it can take up to six months to show up in your system. Shit when I first took my test I wasn't positive. It took some time for me to find out."
"Kendra, I hear what you're saying and I'm really sorry that you're going through this but I don't have it."

I wanted to jump through the phone and ring his damn neck. He wanted to sit on the phone and play pretend, when I was trying to get closure to this entire situation. He knew damn well he had it and he probably had been getting calls from other women too, but now he wanted to play dumb.
"Damn Eric, so that's how you want to play this. You can't even man up."
"Man-up, what I got to man up to. I ain't got the shit" he yelled.
"So where did it come from…I just got this shit out of the sky" I asked, as someone tried to enter the bathroom. I lifted myself up off the floor and the woman came in. At first I was so caught up in the call that I didn't notice it was Toni. She tried to ask me something but I motioned to her to be quiet and lipped out the name Eric. Immediately she hushed and listened in.
"I can't keep on trying to convince you. I just thought you should know, that's all."
"It's nothing I need to know. I don't have it Kendra and I hope you didn't tell my people's that when you called."
"Come on now, I'm not some child. But if I did why would it matter; you said you didn't have it."
"Listen, if you don't believe me you can call up here tomorrow and ask my counselor about my test results.

I'll give her my permission to speak with you and this can be settled."
"You know what, what's her name? I am going to call up there tomorrow?"

I reached in my clutch but I couldn't find a pen. Toni gave me a pen and a small piece of paper out of her purse so I could write the information down. If he thought he was going to call my bluff he was dealing with the wrong one. Not only was I going to call up there but I was going to insist he retake the test, if he had originally been negative. Eric was too calm for me. I felt like he wanted to play a game but I was the one who was going to have one up on him. He thought he was going to live in secret but he was about to be added to the HIV ward.

After writing her information down, the prison address and phone number, along with his inmate number, I ended the conversation. He was never going to fess up and I had already broken my resolution. It was damn near midnight, only fifteen minutes before the Latin Ball was going to be dropped in the club and I wasn't finished partying. Tonight I wasn't about to let him stop my fun. Toni and I had two more clubs to hit up, before going to the afterhours spot and bringing our New Year's in with a bang. She gave me a hug and told me not to sweat it, and I wasn't going to. The truth was going to be brought to life very soon.

We walked out of the bathroom and my Umpa-Lumpa was waiting for me by the door with a drink. Little did he know, I wasn't about to get a dose of any hidden date-rape pills, as they say-I wasn't that drunk. So when we walked by the bar, I stopped and ordered a Hennessy and Coke, and quickly took that down. I needed a quick rush to get over my phone call with Eric and that drink did the trick. As we made our way back to the dance floor, the music paused, and Toni and I hugged each other as we all began the countdown. Ten, Nine, Eight, Seven, Six, Five, Four, Three, Two, One…Happy New Year!!!

Dating?
Chapter 18

It would take two weeks before I found out for sure if Eric was a damn liar or if my life had turned into a scene out of Alfred Hitchcock's The Twilight Zone. Surprisingly, on New Year's Day, his case manager, Mrs. Yassar was in the office. She corroborated his story when she told me that Eric had tested negative upon entering their prison facility, and then she asked me if I had a reason for him to be retested. Without going into literal details I explained to her that I had firsthand knowledge, which made me believe he was walking around with the virus. I made sure to point out that he was a threat to the prison population, who were not infected, and that I didn't think he should have access to infect other prisoners, whether it be sexual, or through some other form of transmission. I didn't think Eric was gay but truth be told, how could I know for sure. I still didn't know how he got it and with all the talk about male prisoners sleeping with each other, I couldn't let him walk around spreading the virus.

My life was beginning to move much smoother but the girls had still been staying at my parent's house. I can't say I enjoyed living without them but it was much easier for me to operate with them in their care. I didn't have to deal with my fears as much or worry about them seeing me break down without warning. I lived a different lifestyle and found much comfort in the glass, or two, of liquor I consumed daily; and occasionally I would take a few puffs from a joint. On New Year's night, for the first time in my life I must admit I took things to a level I never thought I'd reach. I wasn't a drug addict but at the afterhours, which to this day I still can't remember the location, I did a line with Toni. She had pulled out a little snort bag as we sat inside the afterhours, and at first I was embarrassed for her and didn't want her to be seen. But then I saw that several other people were doing the same thing. This was the in thing and although I'd never been a follower; especially when it came to trying drugs, I don't know what made me do that line when Toni offered it to me. It could have been my way of covering up that way I truly felt about the phone call from Eric but either way I had done it; but I quickly realized that wasn't my thing. The last thing I wanted to do was become an addict and from what I heard about coke, snorts, crack, whatever you want to call it, weight loss and debilitation of the body were a sure thing. Surely, that wasn't a side-effect I could deal with and I felt no urges to do it again. I quickly buried that habit.

With Toni back home things were pretty quiet and the only other person who I was in constant contact with was Charles. He had backed off from trying to move in because he knew I wasn't ready, but he still showed a real interest in me. I felt as if we were going back to being the friends we once were, and I enjoyed him calling and talking to me. I didn't ask him too many questions in regards to what was going on with him and Dana, because I didn't want to know. Charles started coming over the house and I felt a sense normalcy as I cooked for him and we would drink a few glasses of wine, before we sat on the couch and ate. I missed giggling with him and enjoyed how he rubbed my shoulders and put me at ease but I hated when the evening ending. It was awkward because I got the inclination that he wanted to spend the night. I didn't know how to ask him to go home and have a good night, so I'd say something corny like, "I'm so tired", or "If I don't go to bed now I'll never go, so", and he'd laugh and leave out. But he always kissed me goodnight; on the lips.

Also Charles was confusing me because if I didn't know any better he was behaving in a manner like he wanted to have an intimate relationship with me; when he knew what was living inside of me. However, I wasn't willing to make myself look like an ass by asking him, when he just might have been trying to be nice to me. I'd be lying if I said I didn't want to make love to him, but I'd be a greater liar if I thought he or I could handle that. I know we'd have to use a condom but I don't know if either one of us could put our fears to rest long enough to reach an orgasm or even to enjoy it. So instead of spoiling our good time I always made sure we stayed on good terms, and didn't add anymore complications to our marriage, relationship, or friendship.

In group we were now discussing dating. There were people in group, including Tracy, who not only dated but had protected sex with others who shared the virus; as well as people who were not infected with the virus. They swore up and down by taking the proper precautions this could be done safely. I had never heard sex being described like a manual you needed to read before entering a nuclear power plant, but then again I'd never had HIV before. I listened to find out if this was a possibility for me but I wasn't sure how to manage dating or sex, because everything seemed new and scary to me. There were websites dedicated to women and men who had contracted HIV but still wanted to have a love-life. I never dreamed of getting on the site, but yes I did browse it a few times, and I found it to be good tool for those who were comfortable with on-line dating. It removed the element of surprise or embarrassment because everyone who entered the site knew it was for individuals with HIV or AIDS who were seeking companionship. There were couples who proudly posted their pictures and then there was this woman's story that stood out. She was infected with the virus and met her husband after she was diagnosed. It gave me hope because if a man could accept you, knowing you had the virus that was real love. Her story, although it gave me hope that having a healthy relationship was possible, it still left me feeling that HIV had complicated so many things for me.

One of our assignments in group was to accept a date, if the man/woman was safe and we had some interest in them. It was Tracy's way of showing us that we still had to live our lives and just because we had the virus, it didn't mean we were dead. We were still as beautiful and important to the world after we got our diagnosis, and she realized we needed love and affection too. Even though she knew some of us weren't going to jump at the idea, she planted the seeds that made you want to live life as normal as possible. After the date, our instructions were to take notes and write down how we felt, what fears we blew out of proportion, and could we date that person or someone else again.

I asked Tracy if Charles counted and she told me no because she wanted me to date someone who didn't know my HIV status. After I had my HIV diagnosis it always bothered me that now guys hit on me more than when I was infected. I felt like they knew I was defected and I would always rudely brush them off. I had actually gotten used to being that way toward men because I had no intention of dating anyone, but I was going to try this exercise out. Not because I wanted to intentionally lie to anyone but because I enjoyed those moments in life when I felt regular again.

Not even a week had passed since we were given the assignment, when I was approached by a guy at a gas station downtown. This man was not only handsome, but he was kind enough to pump my gas and pay the tab. His name was Rick and he was just how I liked them; tall, dark, handsome, and from his brief presentation he appeared successful. He was a real estate broker and was heading to the Reading Terminal to have lunch. Funny thing was that I also was going there to grab me a salmon platter from the Thai restaurant. So we decided to meet each other there and have lunch.

When he pulled off in his sleek silver Audi-truck, I kept telling myself this was just an experiment. I mean I didn't have to say, "Hello I'm Kendra and I'm HIV positive", because this was just a lunch date. As we made our way through the swarming Reading Terminal, we both got the salmon and then found a table. Rick had good conversation and asked me the typical questions, kids, man, career, etc. and I made all of that up. I was single, no children, and had worked as a Yoga instructor-don't ask. It was refreshing to sit there and have this man stare in my eyes and compliment my body. I enjoyed each moment and I didn't ask him much. I just smiled and made sure I was in the moment so I could stop concentrating on my background thoughts. The kicker came when he took his hand and rubbed my neck and said, "Do you know what a vampire is?" If you could have recorded my facial expression it would have been priceless. What the

hell was he talking about? A vampire? Was he being serious or was he trying to make a joke?
"Yes, you mean the characters in the movies with the fangs, right?" I said.
"Well something like that?"
"I'm not sure what you mean when you say something like that, something like what?"
"Well I'm a vampire."

I wanted to laugh but when I saw the seriousness on his face, I knew this joker wasn't joking. This grown ass man was trying to tell me he was a vampire and I thought I was the one with a problem.
"So you're a vampire?"
"Yes I am" he said proudly.
"Okay, so what do you do that makes you a vampire?"
"Well I drink blood and sometimes I sleep in a coffin."

I wanted someone to slap some damn sense into him. He was drinking people's blood when I knew for a fact there were countless people walking around with all types of infectious diseases and deadly viruses. What do you do when someone tells you some bogus crap about being a vampire? I thought about getting up and walking away but I wasn't finished my food; and since I knew after today Rick and I would never see each other again, I just sat there and let him run his mouth.
"Okay, so you drink blood and sleep in a coffin. Do you do anything else vampire-ish?" I asked, sarcastically.
"Yes there is a community of vampires. We meet and get to know each other and invite others into our society. There are those who we just feed from and others who want to become vampires."
"So where are you fangs?"

"I'm going to get permanent ones soon but right now I have false ones, because in my line of work I don't want to scare off my clients."

"So what's your interest in me?"

"With that beautiful vain in your neck, I can tell your blood is one of a kind. I'd love to feed from you."

"Rick, I think you need a new hobby!"

I officially had enough. I didn't bother finishing my salmon and I got up and walked away from Mr. Vampire, as he called out for me to come back to the table. This fool was probably helping the spread of the virus by drinking contaminated blood. He looked normal and by all appearances you'd think he was a regular guy. But this black adult man, a handsome man at that, had a nerve to claim to be a vampire. What a waste.

I wasn't sure if dating would be a real possibility for me. I mean let's just say vampire Rick was actually normal and the attraction was there. What would I say or do next? If the sparks were there was I supposed to walk away from any man where there was a potential for a relationship; and what was the right time to tell someone I had HIV? When was the perfect moment to tell a guy I had bitten from a poisoned apple? Should it be the first time I met him before exchanging numbers, on the second date, or after a year when his feelings were wrapped up in me. This was a discussion we had in group and still no one could give up a definite answer. We deserved discretion but I knew at some point if I was going to take things to another level with a man, emotionally or physically, there would be no way to do that without coming clean.

Dating for others seemed like a realistic option, but for me it was more of an unbeatable game that I didn't know how to play and one I didn't want to learn.

At least if I could be with Charles I didn't have the worry about telling him I was HIV positive. He had been constantly telling me he was going to accept me, for who I was and how he wanted the woman he fell in love with, flaws and all. It was time for me to try and enjoy my life with a man who had shown me that he could be my friend, despite of my viral-load count. And even though Charles had made mistakes in the past, it was time for me to move on because I too had moments where I had screwed up.

A Fresh Start
Chapter 19

It had been a little over a month since Charles and I had gotten back together. With him back home the girls were more than happy to join our family, even though my mom was upset by the move. She wanted the girls to stay with her during the week and come home on the weekend but what would be the point of that. She had helped me but I now had in-home help and Charles picked up his role as the supportive father, and made sure the girls got to school. He still helped with their homework and made dinner occasionally. The house was in harmony and I was happy to be back with my husband, and our relationship, although we were taking things slows, seemed to be progressing just fine.

Initially Dana called repeatedly and of course she threatened to take Charles to child-support court. She also denied him visitation of Prince but we were already prepared for her bullshit. Charles' job had lawyers for the employees at the Post Office and he had been assigned a female attorney by the name of Latoya Smith to help him fight for partial custody. She was very sophisticated, well dressed and more importantly she knew her stuff. She didn't give out any illusions and she let us know the courts often side with mothers if there is just cause; and if they are not on drugs and capable of providing a safe lifestyle for their children. However, she said that in her experience to often men don't put up a fight for custody and even if he couldn't get exactly what he wanted he would be able to see his son.

If Dana would have been a mature woman and put her son first, things could have run a lot smoother. She knew how much Charles loved his son but she was so petty she was willing to sacrifice her son's needs for her wants. Charles wanted to see Prince at least three days out of the week but Dana said the only way he was going to see Prince was by a court order, and then only through supervised visitation at 1801 Vine Street. She claimed she was being this way to protect her son because my virus posed a threat to Prince. Of course her words hurt my feelings. Firstly, because she was loosely throwing around my personal business, and secondly the virus had nothing to do with the wellbeing of her son, let alone my own children. They were never put at risk and I would never see anyone hurt because of my illness. Even when the lawyer Dana called and tried to serve as a mediator between the two of them, she wouldn't hear logic. Dana was so busy talking about me, and she was still shouting out my business and being stubborn. Charles and I knew the process may have taken a few months before we would have a ruling from the judge, but we were ready to get the ball running. The both of us had pressing matters we were trying to address and we were not going to give up without putting our best efforts first.

I still hadn't heard from Eric or his case manager and the last time I talked to her she said she would be in touch with me shortly. I'm sure there are rules and regulations in regards to disclosing health information, but when I didn't get the return call I knew what was going on. The test only takes two weeks before the results were returned, so with it being a month I knew the outcome. He had the virus and now he had been placed on the HIV ward and was too ashamed to fess up. Eric was full of crap but now he had been exposed and no longer could he live anonymously.

Lately I was feeling more alive and enjoying my family, and the constant thoughts of my looming death sentence had ceased. It was all about me and my family and living in the moment. I was still attending group and when I told them about my date assignment with the vampire; it was a source of constant laughter. Every time someone new came in they wanted me to share my story with them. Now at group I liked speaking. Also I found ways to keep myself occupied during the day since I had stopped working. I volunteered at the center, which was a division of The Circle of Care called One Hope. I was a phone operator and secretary, and I enjoyed speaking with people about the services that One Hope offered for those infected with the virus. Even though I was new to this line of work, just being personally affected gave me the compassion and skills needed to help those in need. I was big on suggesting that people come in for group counseling, and if they were afraid I'd tell them about my first time and asked if they needed an escort.

Tracy was proud of my commitment to the organization and offered me the gig as part-time employment. I was happy to accept the job. Monday through Friday I worked from ten to two, and I was paid ten dollars and hour. The pay wasn't the biggest reward from the job because it wasn't a whole lot. Fortunately, I wasn't desperate for money and between Charles and me we were pretty comfortable. Nevertheless it was nice to add something to the pie since I had lost my job at the State Liquor Board.

As I continued to enjoy myself and the positive new turns my life was taking, my love life had heated up. One night after Charles had tucked the girls in; he came into the bedroom and began kissing me as if he was ready to give me a huge piece of his chocolate-bar. I was warmed up, and the juices that had been on reserve all came rushing to the forefront when his hands traveled to my forbidden valley. He lifted my nightgown off and began to caress my body as only he could. The dam broke and the river flowed. I didn't want to stop him but eventually I knew I would have too, but for the moment I was trying to enjoy the feeling of being aroused. He began to kiss on my neck and when he gripped my ass up into his hands and roughly squeezed it, I wanted more than just a tease. His lips began to do all the talking and my mind shut down. He slid my panties off and asked me to show him how much I loved him. Charles didn't have to prove his love to me; it was clear that he had always loved me but I loved him more and I didn't want to hurt him.

I started thinking of all the things I had been through and how my life was forever changed, and I began reaching for my panties. I didn't want my husband to share in my pain, nor did I want his life to end before it was scheduled to; just because we let our sexual desires get the best of us. He looked confused at my hesitation and continued massaging my body. Then he sat next to me on the bed as I sat up and pulled on my underwear.

"Baby, why did you stop me?"

"Because…I don't want to hurt you."

"How you gonna do that? What you got a big ass dildo or something under your pillow?" he asked, as I began laughing.

"No, you and I both know that's not for us."

"Well what's the problem?"

"You know I can't go all the way. I can't hurt you like that."
"Oh, that's it. Listen we can go as far as we want. I have protection and I've been reading this book on…"
"What book?" I said, interrupting him.
"I got it from John. It's about being intimate, well safely intimate with your partner."
"You've been talking to John?"
"Baby, there are things I didn't understand and I wanted to know all I could so we could move forward in our marriage. It's not just about hugging and kissing, I want to make love to you. Damn, I miss you. I miss the intimacy and our closeness."
"I miss you too, I just want to be careful."
"No, you want to be unrealistic. You think people who have HIV don't have sex?"
"I know they do Charles but I'm not sure if I can have sex without giving it to you."
"Well I'm sure you can't. I read that book from cover to cover, and all we have to do is be careful."
"What's the name of the book daddy?" I asked, laughing because one I hadn't called him daddy in a long while, and because Charles wasn't much of a reader.
"It's called '*How to Live and Love with a Chronic STD*' and don't ask me who it's by because I don't remember…but the book is in the middle drawer if you want to see it or read it."
"Yeah, I want to see it." I said, trying to figure out what this book had said to convince him to go all the way.

Charles got off the bed and reached into his underwear drawer and pulled out two books. Then he returned to our bed and handed me the books, as if he had just done a good job and I was about to reward his accomplishments. I looked at both titles and flipped

through the books. I was flattered and appreciative that he had went through the trouble of educating himself on how to be in a relationship with me.
"Oh you weren't playing, huh?" I said, placing the books down on the nightstand.
"Nope, I told you" he smiled, as his eyes lit up.
"Well I guess you know it all."
"No, not all of it but I know enough to know that you're not replaceable and our marriage didn't end when you got that diagnosis. You don't know how stupid I felt when I left my home, my family. I know you're going to be here for a long time and I want my wife, all of her, for now and forever. You spoiled me with your love and there's no other woman who can touch my heart like you do. My girls are my world too. They love me, I know it. And when we all weren't under the same roof it hurt them and me, and I know it crushed you."

Tears hit the bed and the pain of his previous absence began to fall onto the sheets; lifting a deep rooted ache in my heart. I was looking at my man again. He had been lost to me for a minute and life felt confusing without him by my side, but he was making it clear to me I was more than the virus. I meant more to him than anything in the world and now I knew my family would be together again. The love we had for each was not only the road to our recovery but Charles had made me a believer in the true power of love.

"If you allow your heart to open up and receive my love, Kendra I promise you I won't ever hurt you again. I know I hurt you with Prince but I'll never put anyone before you again." The heaviness in his eyes began to release as his tears fell onto my breast. He had placed me on his lap and his face was aligned with my heart, as he began to kiss me and apologize for all his wrongs.

"Daddy I love you" I cried, as I lifted his face up to show him the forgiveness my eyes possessed. Like a love letter he had poured out his heart and I wasn't going to live in my past anymore. If my husband could accept me and give me the respect, commitment, and support I needed, there was no book or person that could tell me that we couldn't make it. Love conquers all they say and I believed in the power of our love, and forgiving Charles was what I was going to do. And as he began sucking on my breast I let go of my fears and gave into my husband.

This moment was different than any we had ever had. I longed for his touch, which spoke to me more powerful than words could have described. I had a greater respect and appreciation for Charles. As his hands ventured over of my body and brought many of my sensitive spots out of retirement, I cried tears filled with joy and love; and I wanted him to take his time so I could cherish every moment.

"Charles I love you. With you I've found my everything."

"Kendra, I know and I'm going to make you feel my love."

"Free me, please Daddy!"

He had gotten up and walked over to his drawer and pulled out a condom. I knew we needed that item and it was what I wanted. I had known all the while that in order for him to be safe we had to respect our new boundaries. As the condom slowly slid down his penis, the latex was now the only protection we had that could ensure he wouldn't share in all of me. My mind and body were put at a greater ease just having the condom.

He continued to caress me and as he begin to enter I said, “Charles please go slowly”.

Charles, the magnificent lover that he was, not only took his time but he made sure I felt each and every stroke. I sung out his name and pulled him closer and closer into me. It was soothing, it was reassuring, relaxing and there was nothing but complete harmony. My orgasm was nothing short than a slight peek at heaven. When Charles pulled out, we both looked down to make sure the condom was intact, and it was. Then we headed to my bathroom and began to shower, washing each other-while smiling and giggling throughout. As we returned to our bed and prayed together, I fell asleep thinking to myself how good life was and how thankful to God I was for the blessing of family and Charles.

The day after we made love our lives had done a 360, like we had never missed a beat. I was really happy and I deserved it. Making love became a delightful routine in our marriage and I had eased up severely with my fears. Charles and I were sharing my previously self-designated bathroom, and we shared our food. I didn’t put much emphasis on being sick. Because I wasn’t sick, I was learning how to live again and enjoying my home once more.

Kyla and Kyra had found new smiles and they got brighter and bigger the more they saw Charles and I interact. They were so happy to see him home and they had begun calling him dad. They really loved Charles seeing them off to school, and when they came home they were happy to see mommy cooking and listening to the radio. I had a new rhythm inside of me. I would dance with the girls whenever a good song came on and sometimes Charles would join. But mostly, he enjoyed watching the view of his wife and daughters having a good time.

I stopped drinking, well I stopped drinking daily and Charles and I began exploring a healthier lifestyle. We went shopping for organic fruits and vegetables and I started taking a Yoga Class at the center. It was good to stretch and practice breathing techniques that oxygenated the blood. The only bad habit-if you want to call it that- I didn't let go of was smoking weed. When Kala and Kyra would fall asleep I would take a few puffs; and it took me a few days before I finished smoking a whole joint. Weed was calming and maybe I had a slight addiction to the effects, but since it wasn't bothersome to Charles and I did enjoy it-I kept smoking my weed wrapped in top paper.

Faced-Book
Chapter 20

Toni introduced me to the world of Facebook. She promised me it was nothing like Myspace; which I saw as a kid's website that basically bored me. I didn't know how much I would enjoy it until I logged onto the site and found its usefulness. Facebook was a social network where you could reconnect with lost family and friends, stay connected with your current family and friends, meet new and interesting people, look at outrageous video clips posted by friends, update your status, post pictures and share them with your friends, network, play games and if you wanted to-you could use it as an internet dating site.

The first time I logged on I was all excited because I had a friend request in less than two minutes, but it was only Toni. She taught me how to navigate through the site, and even suggested a few of our friends from high school to be my Facebook friends. I searched around and found some of my previous co-workers from Market Street and I requested them. My co-workers from the center and Tracy all became my friends. It was a fun site and when I tried to get Charles to join he flagged me. He was on this conspiracy theory kick saying that we were giving the government to much personal information about us and one day it would backfire in our face. I laughed at him and continued to enjoy my new account on the Book.

It didn't take long before I became a Facebook groupie, and at work and at home I spent much of my free time on the site. Toni and I were posting pictures back and forth of ourselves and commenting on each other's status. She was often ramming on someone and posting about how much her supervisor got on her nerves. I told her to stop because if it got back to her boss, who knows what could happen. But this was Toni I was talking about, who couldn't give a damn. She said she believed in freedom of speech and her boss had no business on her page, and besides she had made her page private. I had heard all types of horror stories that made me skeptical about letting outsiders view my page, so I also made my page private and only accepted friend request from people I knew.

Often I'd get messages from men and women who had asked me to accept their friend request and I'd reply, "Where do I know you from?" That was enough for many people to cancel their request, but others- men- who kept trying to pursue me even when my status was clearly marked married, would say they liked my photo and wanted to get to know me. Can you say desperate but what can you say about me, because I accepted a few of them. Sometimes flattery got you access to the Page.

It was mid-March and the girls break was coming up, and I wanted us to go away on a mini-family vacation. We all needed to get away and I posted this question on my Page "Where should me and my family go for a small vacation". I got a lot of responses. I had gone from twenty friends in the first week to three hundred in a month; which wasn't a lot compared to those who had reached the limit of four thousand nine hundred and ninety nine. Toni suggested the Poconos and a lot of other people put down Atlantic City and New York. I assumed they were choosing those destinations based on my Philadelphia location and because I said I wanted to go on a small vacation. I knew the girls wouldn't enjoy Atlantic City because even though they had other activities besides gambling, it was cold in March and they wouldn't be walking the boardwalk. Neither would I. On Valentine's Day Charles and I went down AC for the weekend. After I lost a thousand dollars playing the slot machines and I had no intentions of losing anymore, Charles and I walked the boardwalk. Those damn winds had blown me around like I was fifty pounds. I'm not a lover of cold weather and neither are the girls, so I didn't want to be that close to the water if we couldn't enjoy it.

We ended up going with New York because it's what the girls wanted. They wanted to shop and they loved Time's Square. I tried to convince them to pick another place because it was cold in New York too but they weren't worried about the cold. Maybe I was the only one who didn't like the cold but if they even thought about complaining of the cold weather while we were there, it would all fall on deaf ears. I posted a pic to my Page of the Holland Tunnel, and Toni quickly replied, "I want to go…lol." She knew she couldn't get off work but if she had, this was a mini-family vacation so she was out. My other friends wished us a good time and one of my male friends, who had persuaded me to accept him, had sent me a quick pop-up chat and asked me what part of town I was going to be in. I was ready to delete him immediately because he was showing some stalker tendencies. I mean yes we talked here and there, but there was no reason for him to believe that I was giving up minute by minute information on my family. This was not Twitter and I had no need for followers. So when I rudely replied none of your business, he obviously got my point because he deleted himself.

Sometimes people on the Book took things too far and it wasn't beneath me to put them in their place.

You have to know your limitations in life, and Facebook is no exception. I know the Book gave some people heart because some of the guys that tried to crack on me would have no chance in the real world, or on the Internet, but hey that never stopped them. Then there were the times when I'd update my status and some unknown would respond, like I was talking to them or if they knew me like that to say anything. I wasn't asking a question or for their opinion but they were quick to tell me to censor my page. That would truly irritate me but there was so much about the Book that I enjoyed; like staying connected with my family and friends and that kept me around.

While we were packing for our trip, I got an anonymous call on my cell phone. I hadn't had one of those in a few days. Dana was constantly calling and shelling out her threats like a semi-automatic, but we weren't bothered by her. I knew it was her and I had her phone number anyway, so I don't know why she bothered pressing *67. As much as she tried to force Charles to talk to her, it backfired and as far as her trying to keep Prince away from him, it hadn't worked.

In late February they had a custody hearing and she was told that Charles would be granted visitation. Every other weekend, in our home, Prince was to be with us and then the judge scheduled a follow-up hearing for them in September. She was pissed. I was skeptical about going to the hearing because the mouth Dana had on her would have resulted in a physical altercation between us. If she would have said anything about my illness in or outside of the courtroom, I might have lost it and bite that bitch. But that's why I stayed home. That wasn't my character and I wasn't going to do or say anything that might hurt Charles' chances of seeing more of Prince.

She was also pushing hard to get more money from Charles in the child support court. At the meeting with the mediator, her lawyer had the nerve to bring up my income, which was minimal because I was only working part time at the center. I soon was told by Charles that being married meant we spent more than just a bed. His income and mine could be used to decide a payment for Dana. That was pathetic because he wasn't a deadbeat dad and he had been sending her weekly money-order payments of two hundred dollars. He bought Prince clothing, pull-ups and offered to put him in a daycare center that gave Postal workers a great discount; but Dana didn't want to play fair. She thought my husband was Charles Trump and wanted Prince to attend a private daycare that charged three hundred dollars a week. Then she claimed she needed a part-time nanny when she was home, because she was often tired out due to how demanding Prince was.

Now when he was with us, I never saw this two year old ask for more than the average. He wanted to be fed, he used the bathroom, he liked playing with his sisters, and he loved any Disney movie you put in the DVD player, so who was Dana kidding. She was one of those spiteful mothers who wanted the father to pay them for not being with them anymore. And when she suggested she get two thousand a month in child support, Charles told me his lawyer couldn't help but laugh at her. The lawyer suggested Charles continue sending his payments to her, and keeping all receipts for anything he purchased, until they had a child support hearing in front of a judge because Dana was not going to agree to any reasonable terms.

I was waiting to hear from Eric or his counselor eventually, but I didn't want to answer the phone and get some news that would put me in a bad mood. After we were finished packing, Charles had taken the girls to get some ice-cream from the Acme and some other snacks that we could take for the ride. I was lounging around and the anonymous call kept calling; so I silenced the call and sent it to my voicemail. They didn't leave a message though; instead they called me back again and again until I reluctantly picked up. At first there was silence, then I said hello twice, before listening for a response and then I hung up. The caller called back and I was quiet until I heard the recording.

You have a call from a State Correctional Institution from Inmate 'Eric'. You will not be charged for this call. The use of three way calling and call forwarding will disconnect this call. To accept this call press 5 now. If you do not wish to receive calls from this inmate please press 1 now.

I pressed 5 and listened to the background noise, and then Eric spoke.
"Kendra, I'm sorry it took so long to get back to you."
"Yeah because I've been waiting."
"I know but we've been on lock down because some dude tried to escape and a CO was supposed to have played a part in helping dude out. They had all types of shirts up here, asking questions and trying to get to the bottom of this. So I didn't have a chance to get back to you."
"Yeah, so what's the result?"
"I told you, I'm clean."
"What?" I asked, surprised and trying to keep my cool.

I'm sorry that this happened to you but I didn't give it to you."
"But you were the only one…"
"I don't know what to say for real…I mean when you told me what was up, I was stressing a bit but…"
"Listen Eric, are you sure?"
"I'm sure. I mean if you don't believe me you can call up and talk to my case manager. She already got my permission."
"Okay…"
"I wish you the best Kendra, Goodbye" he said, in a tone that made it clear it was forever.

I heard the door open and I knew my family had just come in. Now wasn't the time to process the information, well I didn't know how to process the news. If I got upset I'd only ruin the day for everyone and we were leaving in less than an hour, but if I tried to pretend-and I wasn't good at being a poser-I'd make myself unhappy. Eric could have been lying but he would have known that I'd call up there and separate fact from fiction. I wanted him to be lying but it was time for me to accept it. But how in the hell did I get this virus! I wanted to talk to Charles but I was scared of his reaction. This could be the straw that broke the camel's back. If Charles thought I was lying about how I got the virus, he'd possibly walk. I couldn't believe I was right back at square one. I knew I wasn't lying but I didn't know where to look for answers. I didn't have any blood transfusions, or I wasn't shooting up drugs and sharing infected needed.

When Charles walked up the steps I did my best to put on a smile, as he walked up to me and kissed and hugged me. We were doing so good and this was just the wrong time for bad news. He asked me how much longer I would be, because the girls were ready to go, and I told him not much longer. The more I tried to pretend to be happy, the more suspicious he became. He repeatedly asked me if I was okay, and then he looked in my face and asked if I was feeling well. The lie rolled of my tongue like poison and I felt bad for deceiving him. I wasn't okay but right now for my family I had to be. Once we got back home I'd have to let him know exactly what was wrong. I wasn't going to lose him again for lying and I would do what I could to convince Charles that I only cheated on him with Eric.

On the ride there I was pretty preoccupied and when we stopped at the first rest stop to let Kyra use the restroom, I asked Charles to let me drive. I felt if I was driving I could keep my mind on the road and off of my dilemma. I wanted to call Toni and let her know about the phone call, and she called while I was driving but this was certainly not the right time to discuss it. With all ears open and no way to talk in code, we had to have small talk until she and I could speak in private.

The drive was pretty uneventful, the girls were sleep after an hour in to the drive and Charles had dosed off too. Usually I'd make a big deal about him falling asleep, because I hated driving with adults if they were going to fall asleep on me. Yet this time, his sleep allowed me to think of many possibilities. When I thought of all the realistic forms of transmission I continued to come up empty. There was no way I should have been infected because I could not figure out how I had contracted the virus. I mean I knew who I had slept with, this wasn't a case of little Miss. Promiscuous and her never ending list of sex partners. I had a crystal-clear insight of who I had laid down with.

When I pulled the car into the valet, Charles woke up and got the girls up. They were pleasant and helped us with our bags as we made our way into the Marriott in Times Square. The girls were amazed at how large the hotel was and Charles kept saying, that's how things are in the Big Apple. He was acting like he was a New Yorker and I truly loved how he treated and spoke to the girls. They couldn't wait to get upstairs and the five minutes it took for us to get a room; they acted as if it had been an hour. Once checked-in, we made our way to the glass elevators and they girls kept saying they wanted to go outside and see the city and buy stuff. They didn't know what stuff but they wanted stuff and lots of it. Now I was feeling like I'd never get off the elevator because it was taking forever to get to the 115th floor. I hated the way elevators made me feel; especially clear ones where the lobby looked as if it was planets away.

Once in our beautiful but snug, double-bed room, the girls were ready to go before our luggage had made it up to the room. Charles gave into their demands and told me to relax while he took them out, and he promised they'd be back in a few hours so I could go out with them. The invite didn't sound inviting because all I wanted to do was drink, smoke my joint, pray, and maybe cry before falling asleep. But I couldn't. Well I couldn't let them see me for now. Soon as they left the room I raided the mini-bar. I drank two Heineken beers, and three of the miniature vodka's. Then I went into the bathroom and rolled up a small joint and smoke the entire joint. We were in a non-smoking room, so I tried my best to conceal the smell by running the air-conditioner and lighting a scented candle the hotel had given us. I took off my jeans and lay in the bed as my rampant thoughts built up a migraine. I could feel my body calling for relief, so I went back into the mini-fridge and took down another two mini-bottles of rum. I then went back on the bed to see how long it would be before the alcohol would assist my body's call for rest.

I felt Charles nudge me a few times but I made no attempt to notice. My body had given into my self-induced drug treatment program. I was calm, tired, sleepy, and not about to walk around the cold streets of New York. The girls would have to wait until the morning. Charles kept talking about getting up and getting something to eat but I wasn't hungry; I was a full as you can get. He got in the bed with me and as soon as he got close enough he could smell the liquor and the weed. He whispered in my ear "Are you feeling okay", and I nodded my head yes and lay my head back down on the pillow. I could hear the girls getting restless and Kyra walked over to my bed and asked me why I had come all the way to New York to go to sleep. I didn't have the strength to respond, I was gone.

When I finally got up out of the bed it was one in the morning. We had arrived in New York at five thirty, and I hadn't done anything with my family on our first day of vacation. They girls were rocked out in their bed and Charles was asleep in ours. I saw the bags from Olive Garden and I quickly went to the fridge to see if there was anything I could snack on. I tried to be quiet but one of the girls had left a huge plastic M&M souvenir on the floor, and the quick jolt of pain it sent up my leg when I stepped on it brought out a screeching ouch; which woke up Charles. It was as if he had been waiting all day to ask me what was wrong and he didn't hesitate grilling me. I had four more days to go in NY before we were going back home, so I kept saying I was fine. But fine didn't cut it. Charles was starting to get

upset and accused me of lying to him, and with that accusation I decided to trust in our love.
"Charles, I didn't want to say anything until we got home but I got some bad news today." I said, as I began to place the bones of the buffalo-wings I had eaten in the wastebasket.
"What's wrong?" he asked, as he sat up and stared now seriously concerned about my health.
"It has nothing to do with my physical condition…it's about how I got the virus."
"So you finally got in touch with him" he asked, as he impatiently waited for my response.
"Yes but it didn't go as planned. He's not infected."
"WHAT!!!"
"Charles, please the girls."
"I'm sorry, come in the bathroom."

We walked into the snug little bathroom and tried our best to find comfortable seating positions to deal with the uncomfortable situation. He sat on the toilet seat as I propped down on the floor. My eyes kept scanning his eyes for emotions and I tried my best to read him but as I sat down, he hadn't shown me exactly what he was feeling. I'm sure he was puzzled; but that made two of us.
"So how did you get it then? You told me he was the only one."
"I swear to you he was. I have been racking my brain to figure this out and still I'm lost. But I swear on my life I never had sex with no other man."
"We back at this lying shit right… after all we've gone through!"
"I'm not lying! I really don't understand what is going on."
"So, you trying to tell me he is?" he asked, looking at me like I was about to lie.

"No, I'm not saying that. I haven't talked to his counselor yet, and I was going to call her just to make sure he's telling the truth. I don't really know what to do next."

"Well until I find out how you got it, I don't know what to do next. I mean a man can only put up with so much, and this lying is not going to make us no closer or help our situation at all!"

"Charles, what can I do to make you believe me?" I asked, hoping he'd hear the truth in my plea.

"Be Negative!!!"

Charles walked out of the bathroom and into the hallway. I followed him to the door and then remembered neither one of us had a key to the hotel room, so I went back to get my keys off the table. When I walked into the hallway, I saw him pacing the floor, partially dressed and outraged at what he had just learned. I mean, what could I say to him? I was telling the truth. I was trying to convince him that I wasn't selling lies by the mouthful and hoping beyond all hopes that this wasn't the end. I had put such a burden on Charles and even though he had stood the test of time, I knew he and I needed to know the source of my infection so we could move on. This part of the mystery was turning out to be my downfall. How could I rebuild without having found the breaking point, and then putting in the work to recover.

"Charles", I called out but to no avail. He continued to pace so I walked up to him and tried to comfort him. At first he pushed my hands away and then he came back and hugged me. I knew my husband loved me and I wasn't trying to hurt him.

"Kendra, I need to know the truth, that's all. If it wasn't him, then tell me who it was and I'll just let this go."

"Charles, I swear to you there was no other and I can't explain…I just can't."

"For myself, the girls and for you, I'm going to take you at your word right now. I just can't be lied to anymore because I can't take no more pain. Our marriage has gone through it and if you're not upfront now, you'll never be. So it's my hope that I won't have to find out no secrets or forgotten lovers."

"You don't have to worry. There is no other person and I'll do whatever I can to convince you. On my life, there was no other man. I'll take a lie detector if I have to."

"No, no, we don't have to go that far. Just understand I can't handle no more."

"I understand, I do, I swear."

For three more days we both did our best to put the latest piece of our dramatic

marriage into the back of our minds and pull together to enjoy our time on vacation. The girls were happy that now we spent every moment together as a family and explored each tourist attraction they selected, before heading home. I can't say for sure if Charles or I had a good time but surely the girls did; and I was thankful that at least I was able to make someone happy. On the ride home late Sunday evening, the girls again were the first to fall asleep and with Charles driving back this time, I joined them. A few times I felt him rubbing my hair and he caressed my hands. So I kept hope that maybe he did believe me and would allow the "Who" gave me the virus to become a non-factor in our lives.

When the week started, I felt better and after Charles had given me a hug and told me he loved me, he left to take the girls to school. I lounged around the house for an hour before I started getting ready to go to work. I had my clothes laid out on the bed, and I only had to jump in the shower and get out the door. I was sitting downstairs watching Regis and Kelly and my cell phone kept ringing off the hook. When I checked my my-Touch, I realized it was Toni. She probably wanted to know if I had gotten her anything, and on Monday's we usually chatted it up before I went to work. Our conversation would continue while I drove to work and once I got there we were either on our Bluetooth's or talking over Facebook.

"What's up girl?" I asked, but she barely let me finish my sentence.

"Did you see your Facebook!" she said critically.

"No, I haven't logged on today. Why what's wrong?" I said, concerned and becoming leery.

"Yo, somebody put all your business on Facebook!"

"What business?"

"Cousin, somebody named Teresa Mars telling all types of shit!"

"Like what Toni!!!"

"Like you got AIDS and how your marriage is over, and that you had to quit your job. You need to check your page!"

Check my page! I didn't even want to log on to see no nonsense like that. Suddenly my other line was going off and it was my mom, but I ignored her. Then one of my cousins called me and text messages started coming in telling me to check my Facebook and get back to them asap. Who the fuck was Teresa Mars? I know I didn't know her personally and why I had accepted her had to be done on false pretenses. I ran upstairs to my bedroom and logged onto my laptop, trying to keep myself from having a panic attack. My internet connection was not moving fast enough and by the time I got to the site, I was sweaty and anxious.

Toni was still on the phone and although her mouth was moving the words didn't register. I had to see what the hell was going on.

On my page, there it was in cyber-space. I had clicked go-offline so no one could see I was logged on while I looked at my page. I didn't want anyone to know I was online looking at this mess. It was all over my page and this bitch had posted the same post to my page at least ten times this morning. People were commenting on the post saying how it wasn't funny, and others were saying how sorry they were to hear I was sick. What the hell! I had twenty new friend requests, along with several inbox messages. Toni had tried her best to combat the post by calling Teresa every name under the sun and calling her a jealous stalker, but she never replied to any of Toni's responses. Instead she continued to post the same post. I clicked on Teresa's name and it took me to her profile page where she had the same post about me listed on her page. She didn't have any identifiable information and she only had one photo of The Comedy and Tragedy mask-where there were two masks, one smiling and one frowning. This was sickening. Toni was talking about calling the cops and all other types of investigation methods, but it was true. This girl did know who I was and she wasn't lying. What was I going to tell the cops, that she's guilty of defamation of character? "How the fuck" I yelled before looking at my messages. I had a message from Teresa Mars. When I clicked on the link her words set the record straight. She wrote:

It must be nice having him for this moment but once he feels the embarrassment you're going to suffer, he'll never stay there. Momentary gain is nothing like winning the war. Wave your white flag, the war has ended.

Dana had done the unthinkable. I felt the tears push through and as I reread her words to Toni, I felt my infected blood weaken and my soul faint. What was there for me to do? Should I call her? What would I say? Was there anything legal I could do against her? I wanted her dead…but that wouldn't take back what she had done. Text messages kept pouring into my phone, and my mom text to let me know she had told Charles. Even my old boss had called and left her a message to find out if I was okay. I had been, as many people say on Facebook-Faced. It was a term used for putting people on blast for outrageous behavior-such as ugly feet, raggedy or tight clothing, or bad hairdos, and never once as I laughed at those strangers did I think I'd be in that bunch. I wanted to delete my page but I wasn't sure if that was a sign of guilt, and if I didn't say something back I felt that was the same as deleting the page.

My old acquaintance called to me, so I walked downstairs for a moment to pour me a tall glass of the strongest store bought Long-Island Iced Tea I'd ever tasted. I added some vodka to the glass because even though my drink was strong, it wasn't going to be strong enough to erase this moment and the events following this mess.

Toni tried what she could to keep me from getting in my car and running this bitch down on site, or blowing her head off. I was so angry, hurt, and yes embarrassed. This was my business, my family's business. I had girls to protect and since when was my health issues to be shared with anyone accept me, my husband and my doctor. Too much was going through my brain and as I so often tried to find that ray of hope, that rainbow after the rain, it was clear to me that not only did I not know who in the hell had given me the virus (and maybe I would never) but my desire to remain anonymous and live what little life I had in peace was not going to go as planned.

The Weight of My Mistakes
Chapter 21

I had to run. When my problems had gotten bad, I ditched all my responsibilities and went to find my sanity. This time would be no different except my location would not be revealed. I couldn't go to Toni's because I didn't want to be found. I was done talking on the phone and when I abruptly ended my call with Toni, I text my mom backed and told her to do what she could with the girls and to let them know I loved them. She kept trying to reach me but talking wasn't on my agenda. What had I done in my life to have my shit turn out like this? Why were key facts still being withheld when I was seeking answers and doing what I could to move on with myself? I had fallen, I had gotten up, but some damn body was always tripping me up!

I grabbed five bottles of liquor that I had downstairs and put them in a plastic bag. Then I took my HIV meds and two bottles of Tylenol and put them in a small suitcase with my laptop and charger. I sat on my bed and put my clothes on, in a trance. As I walked to my car and looked back at my house, I no longer felt as if my life had meaning. My home wasn't my home anymore-it was just a constant reminder of the what-ifs. What if I never cheated on my husband, what if he never cheated on me, what if I never had HIV-that was the biggest damn what if. The what-if's didn't matter because the factual information had taken its toll on me.

As I drove off, my destination remained a mystery. I had to find a place where I could be alone and I didn't want to be found; at least not the way others may have wanted to find me. What could anyone say to me anymore, that they loved me and I'd be alright? And Charles, if he wasn't tired of my drama, I was exhausted for the both of us. Coming into his life was probably the worst thing that had ever happened to him. But at least I could say I had protected him from my ailment and he'd have a chance to be with another women; any woman except Dana because if there was an afterlife I'd have to haunt the both of them.

I rode pass the motel, the North American Motor Inn on City Line and I pulled in but realized it was too close to my home; so I got back on the move. Without a clear target, I soon pulled up to the Microtel Inn, which was moments away from the Philadelphia International Airport. The daily rate was eighty-nine dollars plus tax. I paid cash for the week, to the dark-haired Indian man with the dingy white collar shirt. He asked if I needed any wake-up calls and the question made me giggle. What did I need to wake up for, I thought. Sleep was probably the best way for me to move past this. So I told him I was not to be disturbed as I took my room key and headed for room 301.

As soon as I entered the room, I drew the blinds closed and cut the TV on. My phone had vibrated so many times from the numerous calls I received, that my battery was now low. I didn't bring my charger and I really had no need for it. I opened my suitcase and got a glass and poured me a glass of absolute. No sipping, I downed the first glass and quickly reloaded. I saw a Gap-Kids commercial that had a young girl with deep brown eyes, and I thought about my girls. They were just perfect. Kala who was now 13, and going to be entering high school this fall, had been everything I could have ever asked for. She wasn't the fresh-hot in the pants teen but a young lady who still played with dolls and loved her mom. Kyra, my spoiled brat, that once had a smile that could melt my pain away, was only ten and would need the most attention. I felt blessed and cursed at the same time. I had done my best to make sure they'd never know about my illness. Thank god I had denied the girls from having a Facebook, because if Dana would have reached them, I would have killed her. My girls were old enough to understand what HIV was and I would have had no mercy on her. As a mother I tried to follow the rules and did the best anyone could do for their children. But now I didn't know what was best for them. I didn't see a way that I could continue being their mother with these ups and down. I trusted in my parents and I knew they'd do the best they could with the girls because my time with them had reached an expiration date.

As I drank from my second glass of absolute, I plugged up my laptop and connected to the Internet- thanks to the Inn's free wireless connection. I logged onto my Facebook page and looked at the post again. Exposed, there for the world to see. More friends had made comments requested that I call them. I lay back on the pillows as the TV watched me. Desperate thoughts of deciding the right time entered my mind and I entertained them. I kept thinking if I only knew 'Who' that would be my only escape from my certain death. I had the bottles of pills on the bed and saw my life as real as it ever was. HIV, HIV, HIV positive. I was HIV positive. Not that I hadn't known this before coming to the motel but my life was flashing before me, and HIV was my life. It had taken what should have been golden moments and turned them into a Gilligan's Island and I had no way to get off.

I held one of the bottles of pills in my hand, and then I placed them on the bed as I poured another glass. I was sick on my stomach and I felt I was going to vomit, but I knew it was only the events of the day that sickened me. I cut the TV off and pulled my laptop closer. My page was still getting post from friends and Dana still kept reposting her comment on my page. I felt like crap and went to Google to find a site I had once browsed when I was down and out. It was called 'Suicide Equals Life' and I think I had found the right time to act. On the site you could post suicide letters and ask that they be delivered to your love ones after your demise. At first I found it creepy, scary and even pathetic but that was before my private information was leaked over the Internet. I thought I had it bad at Thanksgiving, but that was no damn comparison.

I struggled to write my letter in Microsoft Word and I read it to make sure I had said all I could say to explain why this was the only way for me.

I never wanted to die. I thought my life was meaningful and when I had my girls, it had new meaning. Finding my husband was the icing on my cake and if I could have died after my wedding, I couldn't have been too upset-But I didn't. I lived only to find out death was on my heels faster than a sprinter in an Olympic race and nothing would ever be the same. No matter how hard I tried, I couldn't get it right. I fought and I lost. Girls if anyone ever tells you I didn't love you because I ended my life, they're wrong! I'm stopping this mess so no one I love has to see me break anymore. I don't want to put you through a week of happiness and a month of insanity and depression. Listen to grandma and pop-pop. They love you and Charles does too. Charles I'm sorry. I want you to know I never lied to you about being with another man. If I could tell you who did this to me, I would have. You've had my back and I wanted you to trust me, forgive me and love me always. I wanted so much but as they say you don't get everything you want. Too bad this time I couldn't get what I needed. Life isn't fair and I learned that the hard way. I don't really know how to end this letter and I don't want to ramble, so I'll just say for me this was my only way to live in peace. No more fear, no more secrets, no one judging me and making me feel like I was the walking dead. I'm finally free.

Whoever ran the site would send the letter to the party you wanted notified in five days from submission, by email or mail. I had put in Charles' email address, and told the site owner where they could locate my body and sent it off. They gave you five days from the date of submission to retract the letter and if they hadn't heard anything by then, they assumed you were successful in fulfilling your plans. It was now time for me to release all the weight that had been attached to my shoulders.

Countdown
Chapter 22

Day One

As night fall crept up on me I had downed the entire half gallon bottle of Absolute, and I still hadn't gotten the guts to swallow the pills. I had them in my hand and kept looking at the label that said do not mix with alcohol. I had four more bottles, which I could pour a glass to wash the pills down but I didn't and couldn't do it. My body hurt and my heart ached but I knew I had to do it eventually. The more I sat on the floor the more intensely I thought if I was making the right choice, but I knew that was only my fears talking.

Day Two

I was still alive and the first thing I did was bring all the bottles I had left onto the floor. It was around one and my head was spinning so hard, I almost fell over when I got up to get the bottles. I poured another glass and began to sip the vodka down and then I felt the urge to just down it, so I did. As quickly as it went down, it came back up all over my shirt. I removed my shirt and threw it as close as I could to the waste bucket and then I lay on the floor and started to cry. I could feel my stomach burning and my eyes went back to a familiar state of heaviness. I didn't want to watch TV, so I cut it off and lay down until I fell asleep. I'm not sure what time I woke up but I had to use the bathroom. However, instead of going in the toilet I wet myself. I didn't feel like getting up so I didn't. I was tired of feeling anything and I wanted to hurry up and get this over with.

Day Three

Last night I took five of the Tylenol pills and drank half of my other bottle of Absolute. I was so out of it when I woke up this morning. I'm not shocked that I woke up because I didn't take enough pills to die. I just can't do it. I went back on the suicide website and read other people's letters that were posted on the site. Some people had killed themselves for reasons I didn't understand. Some guy on there had bad acne and was teased as a teenager and so he wanted out. Was he out his damn mind! I'd take the damn acne any day. I mean didn't' he know about Proactive. There were a lot of people who suffered from cancer and couldn't deal with chemo-therapy and decided to commit suicide because they had depilated down to nothing. They talked of pain beyond compare and how the strongest medicines for pain offered them no relief. With them I had to empathize. There was another note I read, and although I had never known of anyone who was transgender, I could identify with his letter. He was just trying to be who he was. Though he was born a male, his belief is that he was meant to be a woman. He had been so obsessed with being a woman that he cut off his own penis because he couldn't afford the surgery; and let's just say that added to his list of problems by creating new health troubles. In his letter he posted a picture of himself, dressed as a woman and I was sober enough to see he looked a hot-mess. No part of him looked like a woman. He wouldn't even have been able to convince Ray Charles that he was a girl, even if his voice was misleading.

I browsed a few more letters before finding a young mother who was only sixteen who had found out she had full blown AIDS. Her letter stated she had been trying to die ever since she found out, which she said was about five months ago. She and her boyfriend were infected, but his HIV had not progressed to AIDS and luckily her baby wasn't infected. She left her baby on the steps of a fire-station and she posted what she said was the only picture of her baby and her boyfriend, who was nineteen. Then her letter got really deep as she talked about making a suicide-pact with him but she didn't have the guts to go through with it. He bought a gun and as they sat in his car, in an empty parking lot, she was to blow his brains out and then finish herself off. After she pulled the trigger of the semi-automatic and the blood and brain splattered all over her, she jumped from the car and ran away. Because of a petty-theft charge she had been fingerprinted before and she knew eventually the cops would find out she was in the car, so she had to rush and find a way out. She doesn't say exactly how she did it but the picture she posted at the end of her letter is of a bridge and she says-"If your friends jumped off of a bridge, would you?"

I was tired of this shit. Why wasn't there an alternative to my life? With all these advances in technology where was the cure? I couldn't read anymore. I looked at the picture of that young blonde teenage with her ivory newborn baby and I wondered if we were the lost souls who needed help? This depressive state I was in was too much. I drank more, and more, and more, and when I had to use the bathroom I did…in the same spot I sat and rested.

Day Four

I don't care what time it is. My legs feel heavy and I don't want to keep drinking but it's the only way I fall right to sleep. Goodnight

Day Five

...

Day Six

...

Day Seven

I heard a loud knock at the door and someone calling my name. I was so dehydrated I couldn't lift my head and moving required nothing less than a miracle. I felt like I had a seizure and that could have been a possibility. The pressing footsteps were heard as they approached my body and then I heard a voice, which was vaguely familiar. I felt someone moving me and then I heard them as they gagged off the smell that fecal matter, urine, vomit, and alcohol produced. What clothes I did have on were being pulled from me and I tried to open my eyes but I still was in another place. My body was placed in the tub and water was run on me from the shower to rinse of the filth. The water brought a spark of life to my body and I could see Charles with a wash cloth in his hand as he began to lather up the rag with the Inn's soap. The vigorous scrubbing was refreshing and as the water from the shower soaked me, I opened up my mouth and began to drink some of the water. My mouth and throat were so dry. I couldn't get the water down my throat fast enough.

After the much needed cleansing, Charles helped me stand in front of the mirror and helped me brush my teeth. The mirror image was frightening and although I was clean, I looked frazzled. Charles laid me on the bed and walked out of the room. I was still drained, so I laid there with no true comprehension on what day it was, how long I had been out of it, and what would happen now.

Charles returned to the room with a bottle of water and a cup of ice. As he sat on the bed he fed me the ice chips and urged me to drink as much water as I could. He had me wrapped up in a fresh clean blanket that warmed my chilled body. I was aching all over and my body craved some nourishment. The water was helping and eating the ice was the most I had used my teeth since I got to the Inn. Charles started crying and asked, "What am I going to do with you?" The question was rhetorical and even if it wasn't I didn't have an answer. Charles had come back to my rescue and I hadn't done what I thought I was capable of doing. I know I needed help because I had scared the hell out of my family and myself but I still wanted some say on how I got that help. "Charles, please don't put me away…" I begged softly, as he reluctantly agreed.

My mind was burnt out and instead of talking too much I let him do most of the talking and when I needed to I nodded.

"Kendra, what you don't get is that you're not alone. Even in your darkest corner I'm that light that will continue to shine when you need it. I have never been so scared in my life and when I got the email, I don't even want to go there. Just know that no one knows about this and I'm glad I waited before telling the girls or your parents we lost you. Toni's been calling and she's worried sick. Baby, just know that we love you and there is nothing that should make you want to leave us. We are here for you, don't you know that?"

By now Charles' tears were choking his words and I still was trying to regain the fading life back into my body. But for now all I could do was nod.

Road To Recovery, Again
Chapter 23

I found myself back at the house, being nursed back to health by Charles. It had been almost a week since my failed suicide attempt and he was afraid to leave my side. He did all he could to make sure I okay, without taking me to a doctor. At times my mind would remind me of the Facebook disaster and I'd have crying spells. I was nowhere near recovered. Out of concern I asked about the girls but Charles told me that everything was okay and he didn't want me to worry about anything right now. There were some things I knew eventually would have to be dealt with; Dana for one and finding the appropriate way to live with a chronic illness. But I had given up on finding the piece to the puzzle which had been my main objective for the past two years. I had almost given away my life when my time wasn't up. Becoming overly obsessed with an answer that wouldn't change the facts was pointless. And when I accepted that, truly, things felt lighter and my life had more focus.

Out of fear that I was still in bad shape mentally and physical, Charles set up a doctor's appointment and he accompanied me. I had gone back to The Jonathan Lax Center and saw Dr. Reid. I let him know what I had done, and he was more than understanding and I didn't feel embarrassed. That was an emotion that brought me too many problems. I had to learn how to get over caring about what people thought about me. In his line of work, dealing with patients similar to myself, he let me know that suicide attempts were much more common than I could imagine. He also suggested I get myself in a good support group and stay connected with a psychologist. He diagnosed me on the spot with major depression disorder and said before I left they'd have at least three appointments in place for me. Thankfully, he didn't try to admit me to any psychiatric ward because I explained to him I wasn't having any current suicidal thoughts. Furthermore I confessed about drinking and smoking weed because self-medicating myself was not helping me stay alive or heal. He had the nurse draw several tubes of blood to see what damage I had done to myself, if any, and he wanted to know if I had progressed the virus because I wasn't taking my pills consistently. He also informed me that drinking was another way to weaken my immune system. In just a few days my results would be returned but my initial visit showed I hadn't done too much damage.

When we left my appointment Charles took me to Total Serenity Spa and had me pampered. It was a great feeling and I enjoyed the full body massage, the facial, pedicure and manicure; and the salad they served with a glass of freshly squeezed lemonade with chipped ice kept me satisfied. The feelings of pleasure ran all throughout my body but I wanted to get back to my life. I wanted to see my girls and I decided to tell them about my diagnosis. Hiding it was not healthy for me or them and I didn't want them to be confused if I suddenly fell ill and wasn't around to care for them. It would also be better that they heard it from me and rather than an outside source. But I knew I had to be patient because Charles kept telling me I was rushing and that I'd only get myself in more trouble by being fast. So I did all I could to take my time, but it was hard because I was feeling scared-scared that if I didn't do things differently I might fall victim to another suicidal episode.

At my first meeting with the therapist to deal with my depression, we talked about the Facebook experience and the doctor agreed that it was definitely an experience that could have broken some of the strongest people who live with this virus. It was good to finally have someone listening to me and understanding how devastating that event had been for me. Dana would never understand the damage she had done to me and that was something I'd have to accept. Her attempt to get Charles showed him how immature, insensitive and worthless she was. I had nothing more to say about her and as far as Prince went, Charles was only going to deal with him through the court system. I allowed my fear of what people would say or how they'd treat me to ruin my perception of reality. I also placed myself in a block like I was the only person infected, when I knew firsthand through literature and working at the center, that wasn't true.

Even with education and numerous facilities that offered condoms and encouraged safe-sex, HIV has made its mark on the world. In the US it's estimated that there are over a million people living with an HIV infection, and new infections are steady and climbing. Blacks-African Americans are the racial/ethnic group most affected by HIV. They represent about only 12% of the population but are almost half of all new HIV infections. Another alarming fact I learned through living with HIV is that Men who sleep with Men (MSM*)* represent 2% of the population; however, their HIV diagnosis rate is more than 44 times that of other men and more than 40 times that of women. Women of color continue to be disproportionately affected by HIV infections. The rate of new HIV infection for black/African American women is nearly 15 times the rate for white women. So it was clear that I'm not alone and this was an issue that many people are dealing with. I had live with facts and deal with overcoming adversity; instead of giving up. I knew I had the strength in me because for years I raised my girls on my own, and I don't know anyone stronger than a single mother. Now was my time to channel that strength.

As soon as I got home I decided to delete my Facebook page. It was clear to me that some people knew I had the virus and if they couldn't respect me, and accept me for who I was-without prejudice-then their purpose in my life would never be realized. I wasn't going to put out a flag on my porch that said 'HIV Positive' but I wasn't barricading myself in a concealed cave again. I found that my strength and courage was ever present when I was being proactive and doing things to help me understand and accept myself.

That night I called Tracy and asked if she'd be willing to sit with me as I talked to my girls about the virus. She had literature to bring in case they had questions and she was enthusiastic to help me. Tracy was about healing and helping, and I needed both of those things now. I reran the idea across Charles and as usual he was supportive. Sometimes I'd look at him and wonder what I did to be blessed with someone as caring and compassionate as he. At times he was willing to endure the pains I had brought upon his life and I could never repay him for accepting me. He had given me the type of love that with just one taste, not only are you high but you'd become addicted. In my moment I realized if I got myself in order I'd see how full my deck really was; Charles was a winner, I was blessed and there was no denying that.

After the girls got out of school, my mom and dad had picked them up and I asked them to wait until around six to bring them over. I wanted to take a few minutes to talk with Charles and Tracy. Telling the girls was what I wanted but I wanted to make sure it was done properly. We all had to be on the same page and I had to prepare myself for my children's tears, which could easily make me feel horrible and make me regret my decision. But I knew after educating them I could be saving them from what I had to endure, as well as building a closer bond with them.

When my girls walked in the door, my heart dropped but Tracy put her hand on my shoulder and looked me in my eyes and said, "You can do this." My mom and dad instructed the girls to take off their coats and then sat in the living room with us so we could have a family discussion. Their little eyes were curious and uncertain of what would be discussed but they sat, without asking questions, and waiting for further directions. I started the conversation off by telling them how much they meant to me, Charles, and my parents and then I introduced them to Tracy; whom I said was a good friend of mine and she was there to help them understand anything I couldn't explain. I was standing in our living room and the room was feeling smaller than it was, but I knew I had to let go of my fears. I was so nervous that I sat down on the couch because my legs felt like noodles.

"Kyra, Kala, do you know what HIV is?" Tracy asked, knowing she needed to take over the conversation.

"I do", Kala said but Kyra shock her head no.

"I have HIV" I said, and Kala burst out in to tears and she ran over to me and hugged me tighter than she ever had in her life. Kyra, not sure of what it was but moved by her sister's tears ran over and hugged me also, and flooded my cheeks with tears. My parents had also began crying and they were holding each other, while Charles was doing what he could to keep his calm and be supportive to me.

"Mom, are you about to die" Kala asked, because being a teenager she had heard a thing or two, and the typical discussion about someone having HIV was they would die.

"No, girl…my doctor said I am fine. I just have to take care of myself."

She began to ease up her tears and Kala clung to me so tightly she was hurting my stomach. I asked them to listen up, as Tracy walked over and showed them a children's pamphlet that described HIV and ways of transmissions. I knew the information would lead to an onset of questions from my youngest Kyra, and as projected she fired off. She wanted to know how I got it, 'Who' gave it to me, if Charles had it, and if that's why they had been staying with my parents. They were pretty smart kids and I felt better once I saw we were past the crying stage and dealing with the facts. Tracy used her usual charm and even though Kala was taking it harder, because she was at an age where she could understand more about the virus and its consequences than her younger sister; they both were handling it better than anyone could have expected. We talked to them about things we could share, such as plates, cups, and that kissing and hugging me was safe, and we encouraged them to ask as many questions as they had. Tracy also included my parents in on the discussion and answered the questions they had. She also suggested we seek family therapy and explained how that could be very helpful. I let my parents know they had done more for me than their role of grandparents and parents, and I'd be forever grateful. I also promised them that if I was ever in crisis again I would seek help before taking matters into my own hands.

We talked for three hours and everyone seemed to be satisfied and full of answers and suggestions on how we could move forward as a family. Tracy and I made sure one final keynote was addressed and that was for the girls to understand they weren't to tell anyone about my diagnosis, and not for my protection but for theirs as well. Children can be mean and downright spiteful and I didn't want them to be ostracized because of me.

As my mom and dad got ready to go, they asked if I wanted them to take the girls back home with them, but I let them know I'd take them to school tomorrow. I hadn't taken them in so long and I wanted to get back into the habit. I wasn't unable to and it would be good for me to spend time with them and besides Charles deserved a break.

Once the house was emptied and the girls were sleep, I sat in the bed and smiled at how again I had been saved and lifted up. I was lying next to the man who had shown me he wasn't going to abandon me, and I had two girls who didn't run from me and loved me in spite of it all. My family had been perfectly matched and we would get through anything together. I could feel it; tonight I would get a good night's sleep because my yolk was much lighter.

Seek And You Shall Find-Even When You've Stopped Looking
Chapter 24

The next day I woke up extra early and made everyone breakfast. We all sat at the table and since being at my parents, the girls were so used to saying grace that they decided to let me know I needed to wait and bless my food before eating. I had a huge chunk of my banana pancake in my mouth, and when I looked at Charles he had eaten both pieces of his beef bacon; but we both respected their wished and closed our eyes and bowed our heads. It was another moment that would go into the family vault of priceless memories and all around the table there was nothing but smiles being shared. After we finished up our pancakes, bacon, cheese eggs, and home fries, the girls were more than happy to help me clean up. Charles was in a very good mood and smacked me on my butt as he went upstairs to get ready for work. I was turned on but kept myself downstairs before everybody would be late.

Once everyone was dressed and ready to go, we all said our goodbyes and I took the girls to school. This was a good time for me to find out what was going at their schools; and I was clueless because my parents and Charles had been handling everything. With the overwhelming information on new teachers, friends, dances, and recitals I played catch up in the car and I wished we had more time because I missed this. When we pulled up to the school, Kyra and Kala both hugged and kissed me on the cheek, before making their way out of the car. Before they were out of sight, I reminded them to keep our in-house discussion in-house and they both agreed before walking off.

Traffic was pretty clear and I got home quickly. I wanted to clean up the house, light a few candles, and listen to some music before getting ready for my appointment at noon. Tracy offered to go with me today and with everything that had happened, she let me know she had found someone to fill my spot at work until I was ready to return. Based on our conversations, I was sure she was going to let me know when she felt I was ready, because she knew I needed more time than I'd give myself. I pulled my glade honeydew candles out of the closet and lit two of the three, and then my cell phone rung.

"Hi Toni. I know you've been waiting for my call and I'm really sorry it's taken me so long."

"Yeah."

"Yes, I was going to call sooner but Charles told me he talked to you and let you know I was alright."

"Yeah he did, but Charles ain't you."

"I know, and listen, I really don't want to argue and fuss with you. I'm trying to move forward in positivity. I just needed to regroup because things were hard."

"Yeah, I heard you tried to kill yourself" she said, harshly and without concern.

"Damn Toni, if I didn't know any better it sounds like you're disappointed I'm still here?"

"No, I'm not disappointed but when someone tries to kill themselves, I can't see what stands in their way. It's not like you were with someone who was trying to stop you."

"Yo, what the hell is wrong with you!!!"

"Nothing, I'm not the one who tried to kill myself."

"Bitch you are so sickening! I really don't get you but you're not going to ruin my day!"

"That's not why I called."

"Then why did you call because I should have hung up a few minutes ago."

"I called to tell you that you're not the only one with problems. There are other people who have been suffering and dealing with pain for a long time and they don't need to be pushed and bumped to the curve just because you can't deal with your shit."

"Toni, I think you're having a bad day and you're under the impression that you can call me and try to hurt me, when you don't have to do that if. Especially if you want someone to be there for you."

"Kendra, I don't need you."

"Good, well go find someone you need and irk them today, okay."

"I gave it to you…I bet you didn't know that, and I gave it to you intentionally."

"You gave me what Toni? Cut the shit."

"Isn't that what you wanted to know? How you got the virus, right? And my intentions
weren't just to give it to you but I was hoping Charles got it too. But y'all used condoms and it messed up my master plan. But you know what…one is enough" she said, calmly in an insane tone.

I couldn't deny that when I went to Raleigh I had slept with Toni. The first night I had been with her, was one of those nights we were up all night drinking margaritas; after I found out Charles had cheating on my and gave me Chlamydia. She was the first women I'd ever been with and the way she made me feel was like never before. When she first tried to come into the living room, where I had been sleeping and eat me out, I did attempt to push her off but she was so persistent. I was drunk but I remembered the feelings she made my body produce and that was why I kept having sex with her. Her touch was gentle and soft and she could make me orgasm faster than any man or man-made vibrator. I didn't feel like a lesbian when I was with her, and I knew too well that we were related and shouldn't have been engaging in any sexual activities; but every time I was there she was always the aggressor. If she didn't have one of her boy-toys to sleep with when I was down there, I was her first priority; and even if they were there she'd make her way to my pussy after she had put them to sleep.

I was holding onto the phone, unable to hang up on her because I was in denial that she would do this to me. Now that the 'Who' was answered the next question that popped in my head was 'Why'?

"Toni, why" I asked, feeling as if my spirit had lifted outside of my body.

"Oh now you want to know Why, I thought you were after the Who. But its okay I'll refresh your memory. I told you; no I promised you I would get you. You remember when you put me out your house, when you first got with that nut ass husband of yours."

"WHAT!"

"Yeah I promised you."

"You did this to me over a stupid ass argument!!" I screamed.

"No, not an argument, you crossed me and I don't let people do that to me."

"You are fucking crazy!" I said, still attached to the phone and unable to disconnect.

"Well if you think so, that's fine with me. But I knew you'd be easy prey. You're too weak. And I could tell you didn't have enough dicks in your life because you

were so easily turned out by me. Easy prey… like the rest of my victims."
"So this is what you do? You gotta be kidding me!"
"What, no you're kidding me. You're the one who hurt me."
"Hurt you, we got into an argument and you poisoned me Bitch!!!"
"No, I didn't…I just made us closer."
"Wow, you're really gone."

"You know what, you just don't understand. I remember how I felt when I was crossed by the man of my dreams. My dad, I loved my dad more than anyone on this planet. But no matter what I tried to do to show him how deep my love was for him he kept hurting me.

As soon as she came home he was different. He was mean, he yelled and he made me do chores over and over, even though they were done right the first time. He had changed and I couldn't understand why he would be that way with me when all I did was love him.

Every time my mom went away he would fuck me just the way I wanted him to and he taught me how to give him head. I was his girlfriend and I loved it, but as soon as my mom came home he would go back to his mean ways. I hated her. I wanted her to leave or die so I'd have him to myself. She was in my way and the more I think about her the more I hate her. Then you know what, when I turned fifteen, when my period came on, he never touched me again. It was as if I was dirty and unclean but I wasn't. I was so confused and I thought maybe he was scared that he could get me pregnant. I just don't know why he stopped. Then you know he died before I turned sixteen. When he died, I knew it was because he was so torn. He was heartbroken. He wanted to be with me but he couldn't, well not how he wanted to with my mom there. But he died before I could tell him I was going to move out. That way we could be together."

Listening to Toni was nauseating and this was the most disgusting story I had ever heard in my entire life. Not only was I sure she was telling the truth but she had been brainwashed and molested by her father for so many years, that she grew to love it. I was sure Aunt Kelly didn't know what had gone on, because as Toni spoke it was like she was speaking of a woman her father was having an affair with. I had never seen any signs that would suggest my uncle was a damn pervert, and I know Toni was freaky but that wouldn't have to mean she was sexually abused. She was messed up in the head and she really believed she was in love with her father. Their roles of daughter and father had been converted to girlfriend and boyfriend, leaving her twisted; and that's me putting it nicely.

I sat in silence as she spoke but I had more questions. I wanted to know if he had given it to her and who had she given it too. Toni was quick to dismiss that notion, making sure not to place her father, or should I say her lover, in a bad light. She let me know she got the virus from Rasool, the inmate she had maintained a relationship with from behind the bars. He was clean coming in, so it was obvious he had gotten the virus from sleeping with men in jail. She told me how he had gotten caught having sex with a guy in the chapel, and his counselor called and informed her. Toni said she was okay with it because she knew how much he enjoyed sex; and her belief was that he wasn't gay-just horny. She felt that if she had visited him more frequently and had been able to sneak off and have more sex with him; he would have never been driven to men. She was also sure it came from Rasool because he tested positive, right after she found out about her diagnosis. Toni was firm in her convictions and continued to spill her guts, as if she was cleansing her soul by letting go of the very secret she had held in most of her life.

She told me about the woman, Sue, we met on New Year's Eve and how she had turned her out. She would meet women on Craig's list and sleep with them, and she didn't care if they were infected because she knew what she was carrying. I knew I picked up something from that lady but the information I was given now was so surreal it was like being in a bizarre realm. Toni admitted to sleeping with numerous men without condoms because she didn't care about them either. I was listening to a serial-killer speak who had a deadly weapon between her legs and she refused to disarm it. Toni was calm the entire time she spoke, and never once did she raise her voice, which sent bone crushing chills down my body. I had called her crazy before but I had no idea of just how crazy Toni really was.

Toni, my cousin, a woman I had slept with and committed incest with had been the culprit the entire time. Two years of her pulling the strings and laughing at me, as I foolishly went to her for help and thought she and I was getting closer. All the time she was making sure I was mentally unstable and under her sexual control. She had no care for my children, my husband, or my life. I was nothing more than another person who had crossed her, and had reminded her of the loss of the love of her life; her father. Each time I thought of her father my stomach turned.

I wanted to call the cops. I wanted to drive down to her job and inform everyone what she was doing. I wanted to talk to my aunt and let her know her daughter was mentally unstable, and that the diagnosis of bi-polar she and my mom had given Toni was true, but only one of the many issues she was dealing with.

Before getting the virus I knew all about safe sex, and I also knew woman could carry and spread HIV. Even though it was rare it was still possible. But unfortunately, I allowed my hormones to get the best of me because I never took the fear seriously. Well, and I never thought my cousin was going to put me at risk, intentionally, because she was a sick Bitch. There were really no words to describe my cousin and what she had been through, but she didn't deserve my forgiveness simply because she had an immoral father and a gay ass inmate boyfriend. I mean, I wasn't out adding members to the CDC's list of new HIV infections. Toni should have felt some sense of accountability for her actions but her words showed that she had more emotions and concerns about never being able to sleep with her man; which was her now deceased father. She didn't even think of me as someone who deserved to know the truth, or someone who should have been given a chance at happiness. Toni's soul had died a long time ago and she was just a shell. She was cold-hearted and the pain she carried made her a real danger to society.

My puzzle, which I had been unable to complete for two years, had come together and the pieces had all fallen into place. My question, which at the moment seemed better left unanswered, had come to me when I had given up my search. They say when you ask and keep asking; eventually you'll get a response. However, you might not necessarily like the answer. After all my ups and downs, this was the biggest blow by far. This was the Tsunami of Tsunamis, the earthquake of quakes, and there were no more distractions or lies that could cloud the truth. Now I had to figure out '*What*' I would do next…

Message from the Author

I'd like to say that HIV is not only real but with ignorance it can show up on your front door. However, through education and practicing safe sex; we can help stop the spread of the virus. If you don't know your status, go and get checked out today. There is no reason why you should be in the dark when there are many testing centers throughout the United States. If you have questions, The National AIDS hotline in Washington, D.C. is open 24 hours a day, 365 days a year: and the number is 1-800-CDC-INFO. You can also visit the website www.thebody.com, http://aids.gov, and http://www.cdc.gov, just to name a few, to find help and get information as well.

It is never okay to judge or shun someone for having HIV or the AIDS virus. The virus is something they have, not who they are, and anyone can get HIV. No matter the age, the gender, cultural background or financial status.

Before I go, I ask that if you find yourself caught up in the moment, that you remember how cheap a condom is but how stressful and expensive an HIV infection is. Then ask yourself is it worth the risk? Only you can answer that one...

Tiona

Note: There is more than one way to contract HIV, so please visit the websites, call the hotline, talk to your doctor, and make sure you educate yourself!

ORDERING BOOKS

Please visit www.tiona.net to place online orders.
You can also fill out this form and sent it to:

TT-Time
PO Box 44500
Philadelphia, PA 19144-7500

TITLE	PRICE	QTY
AIN'T NO SUNSHINE	$14.99	_____
WHO	$14.99	_____

Make Checks or Money Orders out to: TT-Time

NAME:________________________________
ADDRESS:______________________________
____
CITY:_________________________________

STATE:_____ ZIP:_____

TELEPHONE:___________________________

EMAIL:_______________________________

Add $3.75 for shipping and handling; $2.50 for each additional book.
($5.00 For Expedited Shipping per item)

WE SHIP TO PRISONS!!!